Jiving With a Royal

THE UNEXPECTED ROYALS
BOOK TWO

TOMI TABB

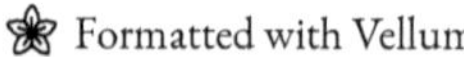 Formatted with Vellum

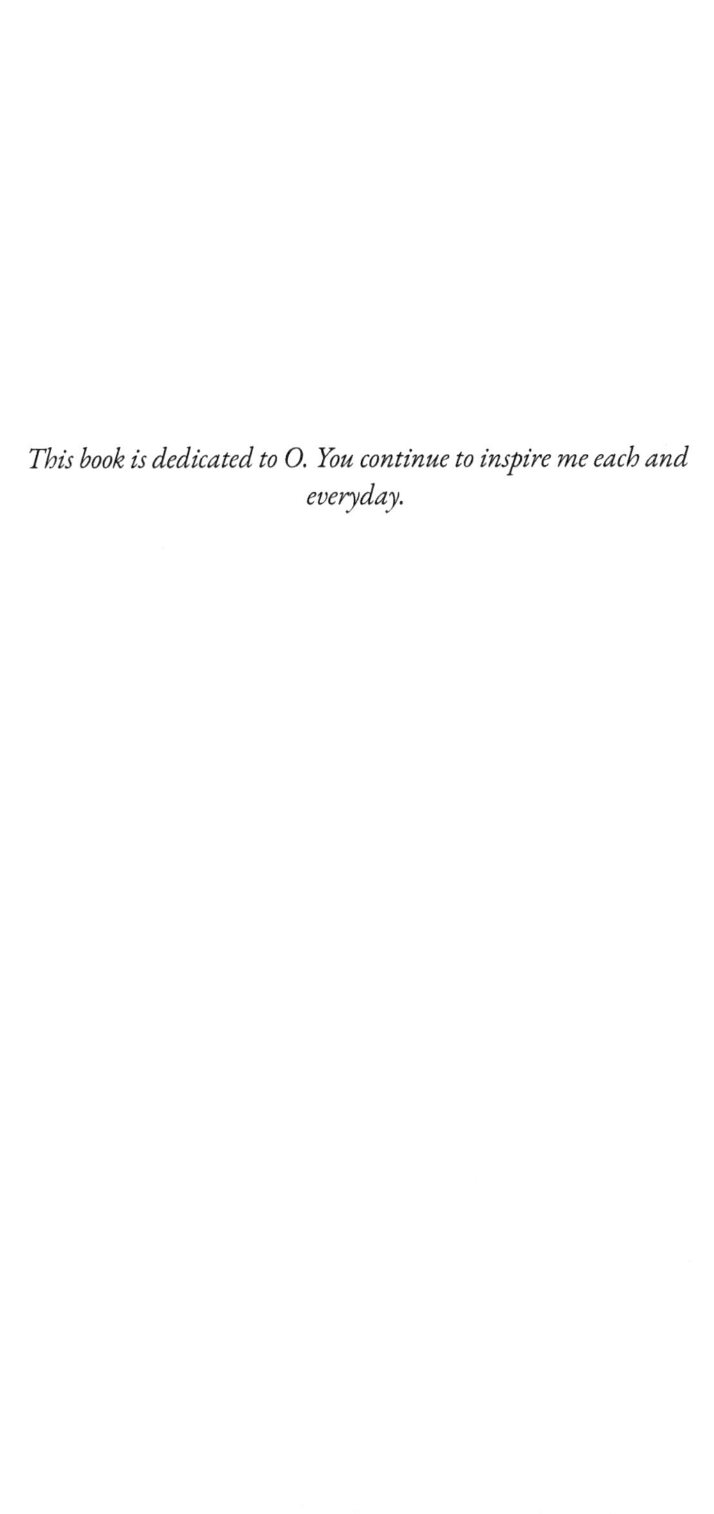

This book is dedicated to O. You continue to inspire me each and everyday.

Chapter One

AMANDA

With a soft click, Amanda Collins closed her apartment's living room door behind her. A wide grin spread across her face. She was optimistic that by the time she returned, her best friend Clara would be reconciled with her boyfriend, Prince David, and making up for lost time. They'd probably even forget anyone else in the world existed.

Keeping David's trip to the States a surprise hadn't been easy. Amanda had almost let the secret slip to her bestie a few times.

I deserve to win an Academy Award for how brilliant my acting was. She waved and bowed to an invisible crowd. *Thank you, thank you. I'd like to dedicate this award to my parents, my director, and most of all, to all of you, my adoring fans!*

Clara had found a good man. She couldn't be any happier for her friend. Clara deserved the world after the last couple of weeks.

A soft sigh escaped her lips. Secretly, she was a little jealous. "David's ruined it," she said to herself. "I'll never find a

"

man half as thoughtful or compassionate as him. Guys like him don't exist in real life, or if they do, they're already taken."

"I wonder what Prince Edmund is like in real life?" Slipping her flip-flops onto her feet and a light jacket over her shoulders, she focused on figuring out what she should serve her guests for dinner. "Clara and David should be easy—they'll eat whatever I put in front of them—but what about his security guys? I'll definitely need more than instant mac and cheese and whatever else is in the freezer to satisfy them."

Opening the note app on her phone, Amanda started to draft a grocery list.

To Buy:
-Milk (soy, 1%, almond, chocolate?)
-Fruit (pineapples, grapes, strawberries, cantaloupe, oranges, Cuties, watermelon)
-Cereal (bran, Lucky Charms, Cheerios)
-Greek yogurt
-Lunch meat (ham and turkey)
-Bread x 4
-Dinner meats?

"Last week, the chicken breasts were on sale. If they're still only five bucks, I can make tacos. So that's one meal taken care of, but I'd better plan ahead and pick up enough supplies for a couple other meals just in case."

Amanda knew she didn't have to cook for the guys, but one, she enjoyed it, and two, she was certain they'd appreciate a home-cooked meal. Her mom had trained her to be a consummate hostess.

"What else I get the most bang for my buck with? Beef, ham, pork, salmon? Are any of them vegetarians or vegans?"

Closing the front door behind her, Amanda pivoted and suddenly collided into the solid frame of a man standing awkwardly on the apartment doorstep. His arms reached out to steady her as her car keys and phone clattered to the ground.

Her head shot up. Before her stood a tall man with tousled sandy-blond hair and blue eyes. "Oh, er… hi… can I help you? Are you lost or something?"

He looks so familiar. A guy like this would be hard to forget. His chest feels like it's a wall of muscle, and judging by how quickly he caught me, he's got lightning-fast reflexes too. Maybe an athlete? An actor?

The man laughed. It sounded like ringing bells. He bent over and retrieved her keys and her phone. "Sorry about that. I was looking for my cousin. He deserted me so quickly that I didn't catch the flat number where his girlfriend is staying. He isn't answering his mobile."

Amanda let out a sharp gasp as it finally hit her. Her entire body felt like it was being dropped in a bath of boiling hot lava. Her pulse took off like an Olympic sprinter. The man standing directly in front of her was the Prince of Wales, Prince Edmund, and her long-time celebrity crush.

How could I not realize it was him?! Say something. Don't make this more awkward. How long have I been staring? Too long!

Prince Edmund didn't seem too taken aback by her reaction. Instead, he perked up and stood taller, reveling in the attention.

Ungluing her tongue from the roof of her mouth, she finally managed, "Er… hi. You're looking for my place. I'm Amanda, Clara's bestie." She extended her shaky, clammy hand to him. "You're even more gorgeous in person." She winced. "I didn't mean to say that out loud. I'm so sorry." Her cheeks scorched. "I'm making this so awkward right now."

Well, that first impression just went out the door.

Ever since she'd learned Clara was dating David, Amanda

had dreamed about meeting Edmund. And now, when she'd finally gotten the chance, she'd made a fool of herself.

"Call me Eddie. You must be Amanda. I've heard quite a few things about you." Her eyes widened in surprise. "All good. I promise," he said, flashing her a wide grin. "Don't worry, everybody is always awkward around me." He winked at her. "Now, what do you say you invite the security team lads and me into the flat before the press discovers us?"

Amanda wanted to melt into the sidewalk. Adding to her mortification was the realization that four buff, attractive-looking men stood on either side of Eddie, curiously watching the entire interaction. She dry swallowed.

Play it off!

"Of course… Come on in," she said, turning the front door's handle, and signaling with her head for them to enter. "Mi casa es su casa."

I'll definitely need to double or triple everything on the list now that there are five more guys here.

"I was just running out to the store. I guess it's good you showed up before I picked up dinner." She glanced over Eddie's shoulder. An idea struck her. "Hmm… is everyone okay with barbecue? We can call it your 'welcome to the States' dinner."

The security team eagerly bobbed their heads up and down.

"Awesome sauce," she said.

Eddie linked arms with Amanda and walked her inside. She inhaled the scent of his cologne. Notes of lavender, cedar, and citrus wafted off him as the soft cashmere fabric of his suit jacket brushed against her. She didn't ever want his arms to leave her. This was her fantasy come to life.

"I like you already, Amanda. But I have a better idea. What do you say we leave the lovebirds alone? You can have dinner with just me and the lads? Do you surf, by any chance?"

Does he intend dinner to be a date? Or is it a non-date? Nod your head or do something, girl!

"Yes, I'd love to have dinner with you, and no, I don't surf. I usually boogie board or float lazily in an inner tube, but if you wanted to learn, I know a guy. I can hook you up with lessons."

"Brilliant!"

Amanda felt herself being drawn in by Eddie's intoxicating princely smile, the same one that greeted her every time she unlocked her phone. At this rate, her face would be permanently as red as her hair. She had no idea how long Eddie was going to be around, but one thing was clear: She had to get her thoughts and feelings under control soon.

Chapter Two

AMANDA

A few days later, Amanda clutched the rim of her boogie board, aimlessly floating in the surf of La Jolla Cove. She smiled to herself, enjoying the sight of Eddie and his security team behaving no better than a group of teenage boys, egging one another on to see who could catch a wave the longest.

Adjusting her own snorkel and goggles, she stuck her head into the water. Below, it was a feast for the eyes. Bright orange Garibaldi fish swam through patches of swaying green seaweed. It reminded her of the first day she'd brought Eddie to the beach. He'd wanted to build sandcastles, search the tide pools, collect shells, and take photos using the underwater camera she'd gifted him.

As she'd rightly guessed, Eddie defied the image of the outgoing, partying prince often portrayed by the media. He was shy, thoughtful, and had a habit of speaking before thinking. Yet what surprised her the most was that so many of the tasks she did in everyday life were brand new to Eddie. She'd known he'd led a sheltered life as a royal, but seeing it firsthand was still a shock to the system.

She popped her head back up above water and glanced back in his direction. The group was huddled in a semicircle, chatting with one another just beyond the wave line.

Two hours later, Amanda supervised as Eddie's security team loaded the groceries into the trunk of their rented SUV.

"Is there anywhere in particular you would like us to place the bags packed with bread or fruit, Ms. Collins?" inquired Jonathan Bowers, the head of Eddie's detail.

"As long as they aren't crushed, feel free to put them anywhere. It's on you if the guys have bruised bananas or pancake-flat bread in the morning," she teased, peeking into the bag. "I hope you didn't try and sneak in another box of Pop Tarts again."

Twin patches of pink appeared on Jonathan's cheeks. "No, ma'am. Three days of Pop Tarts, Frosted Flakes, and Fruity Pebbles for breakfast was more than enough for the lads. They're too sweet, not very filling, and give us a couple other issues." He cleared his throat. "I think I speak for all of us when I say we'll be sticking to *real* foods going forward."

She snorted as Jonathan opened the door for her. She slid into the back seat next to Eddie, who was just finishing up his call home.

"How was the shopping today?" He attempted to sound interested. Amanda rolled her eyes.

"The same as it was the last two times. Honestly, why do you even come along if you're just going to stay in the car? Half the fun is exploring the aisles, and seeing what there is to buy. You might even learn to appreciate shopping if you'd come to Costco with me. Ask your team members. They had a blast eating up all the free food samples," Amanda shot back, a hint of annoyance in her tone. "It would also be a lot easier for me if you picked out what you want to eat yourself instead of me having to call you each time."

Eddie looked up from his phone. "I'm sorry. I just wanted to take a break from your flat. Clara and David are driving me mad. They're so wrapped up in spending time together that it's like I'm invisible to them." He placed his phone face down on the seat next to him. "I thought I was doing the right thing staying behind. If I were to go inside a shop like Target or Costco, it could turn into a media frenzy. I've been lucky to slip by unrecognized so far, and I'd like to keep it that way. Besides, people-watching from the car is much more interesting than watching the telly."

Amanda sighed. Poor Eddie. She hadn't thought about his being recognized.

He continued. "When I asked David to bring me with him, I'd hoped we could do some sightseeing. Knott's Berry Farm, Universal Studios, and Disney aren't that far from here." His shoulders hunched and voice grew quieter. "But with David being so, er… occupied, I doubt it'll happen."

Amanda frowned. Eddie needed to learn that he could do things without his cousin. If he wanted to visit a theme park, then he should do it. People often feared doing things solo, but if they took a leap of faith, they might find that being solo could be pretty darn awesome. Take travel, for instance. When she took a random trip on her day off, being a party of one meant she decided what to do, where to go, and what to eat. There was no sticking around waiting for other people. She could maximize her experience. Unfortunately for Eddie, though, this was something he had to figure out for himself.

As the car roared to life and they began the ten-minute drive back to the apartment, she was brought back to the moment. Buckling her seat belt, she asked, "Any interesting news from across the pond?"

Eddie shook his head. "Nothing noteworthy. It's a slow

news day. Today's headline was something along the lines of 'The Prince of Wales Flees the UK to Raise Alpacas in Latin America.'" He rolled down his window a crack, much to the annoyance of the protection officers. "Apparently, at twenty-one, I'm having a midlife crisis."

"Wait, what? That's the headline in the gossip rags today?" Her body shook with laughter. "I think that's the best one yet."

"I have to hand it to the writers—they've come up with some creative explanations for my vanishing act from London's nightlife scene. But I think my favorite is still that I'm supposedly on a quest to find my long-lost twin brother."

They both laughed. The smile on his face extended all the way to his blue eyes and revealed a set of dimples. Their eyes locked, and her heart fluttered in excitement.

She cleared her throat. "So, er… how are you planning to spend the last two days of your trip to SoCal? Are you okay with having dinner with me again? I was thinking of trying out another new recipe I found for fried rice and pork chops."

Amanda cringed internally. She'd used the new recipe excuse last night too. Did it sound like she was trying too hard?

Their conversation, however, was interrupted by the car accelerating and rapidly changing directions. The burning smell of rubber and the sound of screeching tires reached their ears.

"What's happening?" Eddie demanded, gripping the side of the door for dear life.

"We're being followed," Jonathan replied tightly, his eyes peeled to the outside, carefully watching their surroundings. "Your safety is our prime concern, sir. We're headed to a secure location."

Amanda looked over her shoulder to see a white Chevy Malibu mimicking their every maneuver. The telltale flashing of red and blue lights from the front of the car caused her to screech, "Pull over!"

Jonathan shot a wide-eyed look behind him and assented to her request. The SUV made it to the farthest lane to the right and came to an abrupt stop. The color drained from Eddie's face. The SUV was silent and filled with tension.

She leaned back into her seat. Eddie's rapid breathing prompted her to pat his hand, trying to reassure him they'd be all right. "You're being followed by the Orange County police. If we didn't stop, there's a good chance the high-speed pursuit would be aired on TV. They're probably stopping us for something like a broken taillight, or something else trivial."

The door of the Chevy opened. A police officer in a black uniform quickly made his way over to the driver's side door. Jonathan rolled down his window.

"Hands on the wheel until further instructed," the officer bellowed. "Do you understand why you've been stopped?"

"No, sir."

The officer huffed. "I'll need to see your driver's license, vehicle registration, and your insurance card."

Should I intervene?

"Uh…" Jonathan glanced nervously behind him. Eddie's eyes were wide. The other protection officer in the front seat was on his phone.

Amanda leaned over Eddie and rolled his window down, disregarding the intoxicating scent of his cedar and sandalwood cologne. She stuck her head outside. "Hi, Officer!" she said in her best attempt at a cheery voice. "Look, this is all a huge misunderstanding. Do you see the handsome guy sitting next to me?" She pointed to Eddie. "This is Prince Edmund, the heir to the British throne."

Eddie tensed and gave a hesitant wave. "Er… hello, sir."

The officer lifted his sunglasses and studied them.

Mustering all her charm into her second Oscar-worthy

performance of the week, she added, "You're not going to give the future king a ticket, are you? Because if you did, it could become an embarrassing international incident. Doesn't diplomatic immunity extend to royalty?"

The corners of the police officer's eyes widened. "I was only doing a routine stop for the expired registration on this vehicle. I don't want any trouble. Your Highness, if you could forgive us here in Orange County for the oversight, it would go a long way with our department." He awkwardly bowed to Eddie.

Amanda signaled to him that he should say something. She felt guilty as she elbowed him in the ribs to force him to answer the officer. He glared at her and rubbed his chest. She motioned once more for him to answer the awaiting officer.

He cleared his throat. "We can overlook this incident this time around. After all, you were only doing your job."

The officer's body language relaxed. "Thank you. Would you like me to escort you to wherever you're going?"

Everyone in the SUV shouted, "No!" at the same time.

The officer bowed again and walked backward toward his patrol car.

"You can now officially add 'almost being arrested in America' to your list of accomplishments." Amanda laughed heartily. "Now you know, some police cars in the States are unmarked."

Eddie groaned. "How could the rental company let us hire a vehicle with expired registration?" He rubbed his ribs again. "Don't elbow me like that. It hurt."

Amanda shrugged. "I'm sorry for doing what I needed to do, but somebody needed to take control of the situation."

The unlikely group was now finally on their way home to Amanda's apartment. The sun had just begun to set, revealing a beautiful pink and orange sky.

Jonathan's shoulders hunched. "Sir, please allow me to assume full responsibility."

"Why would I do that?" Eddie frowned. "It's not your fault."

"That's right. It's nobody's fault," Amanda said as the car entered the parking lot of her complex and parked next to her VW. "Let's not tell David or Clara about this. What they don't know can't hurt them." She tried to wink.

Jonathan sighed. "I'm afraid that's not an option, Miss Collins. Leeds was called by Myles as soon as we were pulled over."

"How did he sound?" Eddie asked.

"Agitated," Myles said in a low tone.

Eddie deflated. "If he's called my father, I'm in for it. I don't have the world's best track record." He remained quiet as everyone exited the car and assisted the team with unloading the groceries.

Amanda frowned, mulling over his earlier statement. Why would David care about what had happened? It wasn't Eddie's fault they had been pulled over either. The blame should fall to the rental car company for letting the tags expire. He was giving up too easily, and it bothered her. She wished he'd stand up for himself.

Entering her apartment, the aroma of roasting coffee beans greeted Amanda. She shook her head. David and Clara could drink coffee at just about any hour of the day.

"Honey, we're hooooooooome," she bellowed.

She placed her keys onto the hook next to her door and strode into the living room. Clara sat, typing away on her laptop, resting her feet on David's lap. He tossed the magazine he was reading onto the coffee table. Clara moved her legs without uttering a word as he stood and placed his hands behind his back.

"How was your afternoon? Did anything interesting happen?" he inquired, sarcasm lacing his baritone voice.

Eddie shoved his hands in his pockets. "It wasn't my fault," he said defensively.

"I didn't say it was." David sighed. "Let's step out onto the patio. There's a couple things I need to clarify with you and Jon."

Leaving the men to do whatever they needed to do, Amanda headed to the kitchen.

Chapter Three

AMANDA

A little later, Amanda hummed a Backstreet Boys tune to herself as she danced around the kitchen cooking. Eddie leaned his elbows onto the kitchen island counter, his eyes dancing in amusement. "Do you know the dance steps from every single nineties music video?"

"Nope. Not every one. Just the moves from a couple NSYNC and Backstreet Boys videos."

Eddie rolled his eyes. "Close enough."

The oven timer chimed. Amanda pulled open the door and extracted the glass Pyrex containing the pork chops. The scent of fresh meat wafted through the air.

"Perfect."

Eddie's eyes widened. He licked his lips. "This looks like something out of a food magazine or a show like *The Great British Bake Off*."

"I'll take that as a compliment." Peeling off her oven mitts, she pointed out to Eddie where she wanted the plates and utensils placed. "I got the recipe from a book I picked up at a used bookstore. I swear, vintage cookbooks have the best ideas. The recipes are classic for a reason."

He stood and collected the items she was requesting. "I feel guilty that you've been doing so much cooking since we've been here."

Amanda brushed him off. "Don't be. I *love* it. Grandma Collins and I used to spend hours together in the kitchen when I was growing up. These days, I don't get much of a chance to keep my skills sharp. I'm always working." She cringed. "It kills me that most of the time I end up eating frozen meals just because they're quick to make and have a long shelf life."

She surveyed their handiwork. Containers of green salad, side veggies, fried rice, and the pork chops were lined up in a neat row on the island. Steam rose from the meat.

"Would you like me to prep a plate for each of us before we call the lads in?" Eddie's gaze drifted toward the living room.

"Yes, please. While you do that, I'll take care of the drinks." She stretched up to the cabinet and removed two glasses.

"Water for me, please," Eddie said.

"You and I are eating out on the terrace tonight. It's too nice to be indoors."

She'd made up her mind. Tonight, she was going to seize the opportunity and have dinner alone with Eddie. She didn't know if she'd have another chance.

"Brilliant."

The moment Eddie indicated he'd finished fixing their plates, Amanda put her fingers to her lips and let out a shrill whistle. In a matter of moments, three on-duty and two off-duty security team members materialized from the living room and lined up.

"Enjoy your dinner, boys." Amanda saluted the line.

They replied with a chorus of "Thank you."

Taking Eddie's hand, she led him outside and slid her patio

door shut. David and Clara could fend for themselves. She had no idea what they were up to anyway.

They settled into their seats across from one another. Hearing the steady traffic from the street behind them, Amanda pulled out her phone, and opened her Spotify app. Glancing at the screen, she asked, "Is Queen okay with you?"

He leaned back, rolling his head side to side to release the tension from his shoulders. "Brilliant."

She set her phone on the railing, and Freddy Mercury's voice filled the silence between them. The terrace, though small, held enough space to fit a round white patio table and two plastic chairs. A planter box full of leaf matter and dirt adorned the railing opposite the patio door. Amanda had relatively little luck in keeping plants alive with her chaotic schedule.

Come Monday, the vacation is over, and it's back to work. But I still have two days. Until then, I'm going to soak up every moment I can with Eddie. Let's see… what can I bring up tonight that we haven't talked about yet? Maybe cars?

At first, she'd thought it might be challenging to block out the information she already knew about him, but as she was finding out, it wasn't. The items on the internet about Eddie's likes and dislikes weren't accurate. Every time they talked, she learned something new about him.

"So the show we had on last night, *Top Gear*. Is that one of your favorite programs?"

Eddie's eyes lit up, the corners crinkling in delight. He leaned forward, using his hands to animate his explanation about his classic Jaguar and Bentley collection as they enjoyed their dinner.

Ding. Ding. Ding. Cars is a winner.

"And how did you get so interested in cars?"

"My grandfather on my mum's side. He worked on them during the war and took to assembling motors for fun. His garage was always chock-full of the odd automobile parts. Grandmum was always nagging him to downsize his collection." He chuckled.

"My grandad was like that too, only it was airplanes instead of cars."

Eddie's eyes widened. "Airplanes?"

"Yup. My grandad on my dad's side was a pilot. He even had a Stearman biplane. Flying literally runs in my blood."

"Fascinating."

Eddie shared that his grandad had left him his vintage car collection, and that someday, he hoped to learn how to properly restore them.

All too quickly, they finished the main course. "That recipe is another hit with me, Collins. When I get home, I'll have to have a tailor let out all my clothes from all the weight I'm putting on." Eddie patted his flat stomach.

She seriously doubted that. Her gaze momentarily traveled to the outline of defined abs peeking through the fabric of his fitted T-shirt.

Taking advantage of the change in subject, Amanda casually brought up, "So what did you and David discuss earlier? You were gone a long time."

Eddie shrugged. "I don't have anything to hide. David just wanted to know exactly what happened with the police."

Amanda nodded. "He knows it wasn't your fault, right?"

"Yes." Eddie's attention turned to his napkin.

"I sense a but…"

He sighed. "But I thought he was still going to blame me."

Amanda tilted her head to the side. "And why is that?"

"Because of how I used to be."

She began gathering their plates and utensils. "Is that why you froze in the car?"

Eddie nodded. "Seeing the police today triggered some particularly nasty memories I'm keen to forget. I've been working hard to prove that I'm on my way to being a reformed prince and that I'm not a partying playboy. I've been trying my best to start taking on more responsibilities."

Amanda absorbed the information.

"A couple of weeks ago was the first time I could ever remember my father telling me that he was proud of me," Eddie shared, lifting his chin. "Hearing those few simple words filled me with so much joy. I want to keep being a son who my dad continues to be proud of and not an embarrassment to the family."

"Oh, Eddie, I think your dad will always be proud of you, no matter what."

"Perhaps." He rubbed the back of his neck. "Let me help you with those." Eddie popped up to his feet.

"I've got it."

"No, I insist." He took the plates, utensils, and glasses from her hands. As he stood next to her, she felt the heat rolling off his body. "You know, Collins, I was impressed by you earlier today. You're so spunky and fearless."

She slid the patio door open for him. "Don't forget to add to your list that I'm an excellent cook."

"We've already established that." Walking over to the sink, he set the items down. Spinning around, he gently took hold of her hand and gazed into her eyes. A jolt of electricity shot through her body. Her pulse began to quicken.

"Collins, you make me feel like a regular old bloke. I've enjoyed spending the last week with you more than you know. Do you think you can see yourself being a friend to an alpaca-farming Prince of Wales?"

Amanda's heart fluttered. A smile tugged at her lips. "Absolutely, Princey. But just to be clear, now that you've asked me to be your friend, you won't be able to take it back. You'll be stuck with me."

Eddie laughed. "Noted."

You have no idea how happy you're making me right now. I've always had the world's largest crush on you. Having you as a friend is one of my wildest fantasies come true.

Eddie grinned. "How about we celebrate with dessert? I can send one of the guys out for some ice cream."

Amanda sauntered over to the freezer. "No need. I made vanilla-bean cake pops."

"Collins, you might've just replaced David as my all-time favorite person."

She giggled. "Just for that, you can have first dibs."

Eddie pumped his fist and helped himself to a cake pop. "Thank you." He kissed her on the cheek. Her body hummed in delight. All her limbs felt weightless.

Clearing her throat, she called out, "Boys! It's dessert time."

She heard the sound of several grown men excitedly returning to the kitchen.

"Dessert too? You spoil us, Miss Collins. Let us know when you're done in here and we'll start on the washing up," Jonathan said.

"I will."

Friends with a prince and an army of men to do the dishes and clean my kitchen. I'm living in a perfect world right now. Can't get better than this.

Chapter Four

EDDIE

As she drove, Amanda belted out the words from the chorus of "Surfin' USA" by the Beach Boys, loud and off-key.

Covering his ears, Eddie wondered if he might be able to pop the door open and make a run for it. One of the personal protection officers, or PPOs, in the back of the car chuckled and, as if reading Eddie's mind, offered, "I wouldn't recommend it, if I were you."

The signal they were stopped at turned green. Amanda put the pedal to the metal and zoomed along the Pacific Coast Highway faster than the posted speed limit. Eddie gripped the sides of the car and said a silent prayer. He wasn't getting any more used to her need for speed. At least when he drove fast, it was on a racecourse.

When Amanda comes to London, I'm going to insist on choosing the music and being the driver.

"Thank you, thank you." She mock bowed to the nonexistent applause as the song ended.

Everyone in the car exhaled a collective sigh of relief when Amanda's CD ejected itself from the player.

"Oh bummer, that must've been the last track on my *Greatest Hits of the Beach Boys* CD. Should we start it over again?" she asked with a glint of mischief on her face.

"No!" Eddie and his two protection officers exclaimed at the same time.

"Oh, come on. My singing wasn't that bad." She pouted, then jerked the car to a sudden stop as the next signal changed to red.

Eddie wasn't exactly sure how to answer this one. Should he lie and tell her it was amazing, or bluntly tell her it was awful?

I better be honest.

"Actually, it was pretty rancid. I think I've heard better shower singing from David," Eddie said matter-of-factly, bracing himself.

Although they were still in the early stages of developing their friendship, he was growing increasingly confident in his ability to banter with Amanda.

"Ha! I won the bet! You owe me lunch, Jonathan!" she exclaimed, glancing into the back seat of the car. Amanda did a full-blown Usain Bolt pose in her driver's seat. "Victory is mine."

Eddie raised an eyebrow. Just what was going on? Why was his chief PPO pulling out his wallet and handing her a fifty-dollar bill?

Eddie crossed his arms. "Does someone care to share what just happened?"

Amanda shrugged, her eyes staying focused on the road as the signal turned green.

"We had a bet that you would tell Ms. Collins her singing was well done instead of being honest with her," Jonathan muttered.

"I should have known this was a joke," Eddie moaned.

If there was one thing he admired about Amanda, it was

her approach to their relationship. She valued honesty, no matter what. It was a two-way street, and he fully appreciated that. There were enough yes-men around him.

Eddie was quickly growing attracted to this outspoken, fun-loving American. She was the only person, aside from David, with whom he could chat for hours at a time about the most random subjects.

This was his third trip to America in the last few months since meeting her, all aimed at finalizing ten million pounds in donations for the Waleeds Trust from several A-list British celebrities in Hollywood.

He could've left the details for David to sort out, but visiting California meant spending time with Amanda. When they were together, it meant he could temporarily step away from royal life and could just be Eddie. Now, if he could get her to drive at the speed limit, everything would be perfect. Or was her speedy driving part of the bet too?

The car jerked once again. *No, this is normal, Collins-style driving.*

Amanda aggressively sped up, cut over two lanes, and signaled a turn into the beach parking lot. Just as a car was pulling out, she managed to secure a parking spot steps away from the Crystal Cove State Park beach trailhead and her favorite restaurant.

The salty scent of the beach below the restaurant wafted up to them. Eddie had to admit, each time he traveled to California, he eagerly anticipated spending time at the beach. As Amanda brought the car to a stop, his stomach rumbled.

Were they planning to go inside to dine? He'd need to put a shirt on if they were. Wearing only damp board shorts and flip-flops wouldn't pass muster.

Amanda turned the ignition off. "All right everyone, time for lunch at the BBQ Shack. I hope you've worked up an appetite after all that surfing at Sunset Beach. After lunch, we'll explore the tidal pools here at Crystal Cove, followed by dinner, grilled by Jon. Today's my day off from cooking."

Eddie and his team smiled. Food was just what they needed after their morning adventure. He stepped out of the car and stretched his legs. His muscles were beginning to cramp from overuse. "Collins, I like you, but my team does the driving from now on whenever I'm in town. I am never letting you chauffeur me again. You scared the daylights out of me."

She wisely chose not to comment and tossed a plain blue cotton shirt at him. "Put this on, just in case."

Jonathan jogged up to the restaurant for a security check while Amanda rolled up the top of her convertible.

"Come on, at least I didn't drive on the other side of the road like you did this morning," she shot back as she slid out of the car.

A light breeze blew past, and seagulls circled overhead, crying out and scouting for scraps of food either left by beach-goers or from the restaurant. Eddie gazed out at the seashore below, where the waves gently broke out over the sand. At the other end of the parking lot, a black SUV with the rest of his detail found a parking spot. Eddie and Amanda strolled over to it.

A minute later, Jonathan returned with a grim expression. "It's crowded. You two will have to eat lunch in the car. The same order as last time?"

"Yes," they both affirmed.

"Chaps?"

The other officers nodded.

"Back in ten."

As Jonathan started toward the takeaway restaurant, Amanda added, "Don't forget the Neapolitan milkshakes!"

Without turning around, Jon held up his hand in acknowledgment.

"Back to your Jetta?" Eddie asked.

"Looks that way."

I'm lucky Amanda understands the need for low-key outings and discretion.

Settling into the back seat, she rested her head against the window. "So, I didn't get a chance to ask you earlier, but are you ready for basic training?"

"Physically, I think so." Eddie blinked slowly. "David's pushed me hard these last few weeks. I'm probably in the best physical shape of my life. Mentally, I'm not so sure."

"What's worrying you?"

"The reaction of the other recruits to having me in their platoon." Eddie opened his window. The cool air hit his face. "David's made it clear to me that during basic the sergeant instructors will ensure everyone is treated the same, but I still have doubts."

"Such as?"

"I'll be under a microscope with both army leadership and my fellow recruits. Will I be able to adapt to the military lifestyle? Will I ever be able to fit in? The last thing I want to do is cause any unnecessary tension among my fellow recruits."

"Eddie, you'll manage just fine, trust me," Amanda reassured, resting a hand on top of his. "Have some faith in yourself and trust that things will work out. There's no point in stressing about things you can't control." She arched her eyebrow. "What's my favorite saying?"

A goofy grin crossed his face. "Hakuna matata."

"Which means?"

"No worries."

"Exactly." She poked him in the chest. "Words to live by."

Amanda confused him every time he interacted with her. He studied her as she wrestled to tame her frizzy and unruly curly red hair into a ponytail. The way she pouted her lips and wrinkled her nose struck him as endearing. She intrigued him. She was a woman who traveled the world weekly and had no problems saying whatever was on her mind.

I wish I were as confident as Amanda. She fully embraces and owns who she is.

Their friendship was purely platonic, but could there be a hint of something more? They'd officially been friends for three months. More and more, when he was alone, his thoughts turned to Amanda.

I want us to be more than friends, but I also don't want to risk ruining what we have.

Eddie inhaled sharply as he felt the weight of Amanda's head leaning into his chest, catching him off guard. Her loose hairs tickled his nose. Did he smell strawberries? Her hands played with the rim of his shirt. She was warm. Tentatively, he brushed his hand on her arm, and she shivered. Her skin was silky soft.

"Driving is exhausting work." She sighed and let out a yawn. "I'm so tired. Luckily, you make the perfect pillow."

Just as he'd relaxed and started to enjoy the sensation of having Amanda rest on him, a knock on the window brought Eddie back to reality. He groaned internally and rolled the window down. Jon passed them two milkshakes, cheeseburgers, and a basket of chips for them to share. He couldn't bring himself to call them fries.

Amanda perked up and breathed in the scent of the food. *She looks so happy right now. Food is the way to her heart.*

Each with a tray in hand, they tucked into their food. "Bon appétit," he wished her.

Eddie had to admit, there was something about the BBQ Shack's food that he couldn't resist. He shoved a handful of chips into his mouth. They were crunchy and perfectly salted.

Maybe I should consider opening a BBQ Shack franchise in

London if my military career doesn't pan out. I could live off this food.

They ate voraciously. The only sound in the car was the crinkle of wrappers and slurping of their milkshakes.

"Delicious." Eddie sucked up the last bit of his milkshake. "I'm going to miss this. By this time next week, I'll be relegated to army food."

"That's right. Who knows when your next trip to Cali is going to be." Amanda's gaze rested on his face for a moment. "I'll have to visit you."

"You'd be willing to do that?"

"You bet. We're friends, aren't we?"

He scratched his chin. "Yes, but traveling all the way to the UK is a lot to ask of you."

"Not really. Remember, I'm a flight attendant," she said, pointing to herself. I travel through London all the time."

"I know that look… what are you thinking?" He could practically see the wheels in her head spinning in overdrive.

"We need to squeeze in one more SoCal experience before you leave for the army. How do you feel about playing tourist at Disneyland tomorrow?"

Eddie dry swallowed. "I'd love to, except it's too much of a security risk."

He'd given up on visiting the world-famous theme park weeks ago. As long as he was able to spend the last day of his trip at Amanda's place, hanging out and watching *Top Gear*, he'd be happy.

"I have a plan. I just need to know if you're game," she said, placing her rubbish on top of the empty tray.

Eddie's lone security team member in the car with them stayed quiet. He wondered if the lads were already aware of what she had planned for him.

"Provided Jon agrees, it's a yes from me. I've always wanted to go."

"I had a very intriguing chat with Jon last night. All you have to do is trust me. I have a full-proof plan."

Amanda's cheesy grin terrified Eddie even more than her driving skills earlier in the day.

That's what I'm afraid of.

Chapter Five

AMANDA

"I would've brought a bucket and shovel with us if I'd known you intended to collect so many shells." Eddie laughed as he and Amanda strolled barefoot down the beach, their hands linked.

Amanda continued to stuff anything that didn't appear too broken into the pocket of Eddie's hoodie. As he walked, the shells clicked together. The afternoon sun bathed them in a golden light. There were relatively few other people out and about.

"No need for those when you've got a perfectly good pocket." Amanda placed one last shell into the bulging center pocket. "There. That should be enough for my housewarming project for Clara."

"What are you going to make?"

"I'm gonna take a glass bottle, fill it with some sand, shells, and a piece of driftwood I found. It'll remind of her SoCal if she gets homesick."

The waves, now choppier than before, hinted at an impending tide change. They stepped out into the water, letting nature's foot spa massage their feet.

"You've got a pretty high pain tolerance for walking on a beach with so much rock and shell debris. If I weren't used to it, I wouldn't be able to do it," Amanda remarked.

Eddie shrugged. "It's not so bad." His eyes scanned the horizon, focusing on some intriguing rock formations. "Do you think we have enough time to go climb and explore some of those caves you were talking about yesterday?"

"Sorry, Princey, but there isn't enough daylight for us to get there and back." Amanda laughed and shook her head. "Plus, I think your team would hate me even more than they do now, after all the physical energy y'all spent this morning."

The pair glanced at the two protection officers behind them. From their body language, she knew they were relieved not to have to put up with any more of her scheming today.

Speaking of which, we need an early start tomorrow.

A cool breeze began to blow, and Amanda shivered. She ran her hands over her arms to try and retain a little of the afternoon warmth. Eddie silently slipped his hoodie off and placed it over her shoulders. It was nice and warm from his wearing it.

"Watch the shells," she joked

Eddie wore a long-sleeved rash guard, but Amanda could make out a few goose bumps on his arms. Pulling the sweatshirt closer to her body, she caught the scent of their lunch.

"Are you ready to call it a day? I certainly wouldn't mind a cozy night in at your place. Today's beach-going has taken more energy out of me than I anticipated," Eddie admitted.

I wonder what he has in mind for a night in.

Her thoughts raced through a million and one different scenarios. Her face flushed as she imagined Eddie spending the night at her place instead of his posh hotel, just one room over from her. Butterflies fluttered in her stomach.

The more time she spent in Eddie's presence, the more addicted she became to finding ways for him to participate in new adventures. He was gradually shedding his reserved exterior, and as she peeled back the layers, she was beginning to understand Eddie on a deeper, more intimate level.

He was a man she considered a close friend and confidant. She was drawn in by his kindness, his humor, and his newly discovered passion to make a difference in the world through charity work.

She found herself daydreaming about what it would be like to share more than just friendship with Eddie, to explore a romantic connection that went beyond the surface. She held a hope their friendship could blossom into something more profound and beautiful. But would he ever feel the same way?

"You're reading my mind, Sherlock." Turning to the team behind her, she yelled, "Time to head home guys." They turned tail and started back to the beach parking lot. "Are you all right if we play the Beach Boys again on the way home?"

Eddie didn't answer her immediately. He ran a hand through his hair. "Only if I get to sing along as loudly as you. When you next come to London, it'll be my turn to indoctrinate you with some good old classic British rock."

Amanda handed her phone to him. "Tell you what. I'll let you pick the tunes for the drive back. Choose wisely. I judge a person a lot based on music selection."

Eddie laughed. "Challenge accepted. Let's begin with The Who."

Eddie had to be woken up in the wee hours of the morning in order squeeze in a workout before they left for Disneyland's opening rope drop. Amanda shook her head at the contorted sleeping position of her prince. She stood in the doorway of the guest room, gazing at him.

Eddie slept with one foot stuck out from underneath the

covers and his head hidden beneath the pillow, with his arms around it as if he were swimming. She enjoyed the sight of seeing him sleep shirtless, wearing only basketball shorts. Already solidly lean-muscled, Amanda estimated that he had put on about ten pounds of muscle since his first trip to California.

How does he function? He's like a human pretzel. I swear, if I slept like that, I wouldn't walk normally for like a week. Plus, he seems to sleep through anything. Maybe he's taken contortion lessons from Clara.

Amanda, used to irregular hours as a flight attendant, had an array of teas and coffees ready for the members of Eddie's detail, who'd spent the night in her living room. She had done her best to keep the noise levels down while working in the kitchen, but it still woke them. She supposed being a light sleeper was in their job description.

She tiptoed into the room and set a cup of tea and a muffin next to Eddie's phone on the nightstand, out of the reach from any flailing limbs. Then, without any warning, she pounced onto the only unoccupied space on the guest bed.

"Wake up! Wake up! Wake up!" she exclaimed. Eddie, not fully awake, half-heartedly threw a pillow at her. "Missed me!" she chirped.

Eddie pulled the remaining pillow back over his head and groaned. After another playful bounce from her, he stirred and brought his phone close to his face. Checking the time, he complained, "It's three a.m. in the bloody morning. I only need about an hour to get ready. Why are you waking me up now?"

"You're the one who mentioned going for a run. We need to leave at six to be in Anaheim by seven to snag a good parking spot. I'm not driving, so we need all the extra time we can get," Amanda retorted.

"Fine," Eddie grumbled, moving slowly toward the tea and muffin. "Thank you for breakfast."

"Your guys have the gym cleared out for you. Just throw your shoes and shirt on and get moving. If you want a shower, I'll leave some towels outside the bathroom." Amanda started humming a Disney tune.

Eddie sat up straighter and rubbed his eyes. He sniffed the steaming beverage. "Is this Earl Grey?"

"Of course! Now just make sure you shave. The makeup for your disguise applies much smoother if your stubble isn't too thick," she called over her shoulder as she left the room, positive he hadn't processed what she just said.

If Clara were still around, Amanda would have preferred to use her bestie's superior makeup-applying skills. Two months ago, however, she'd made the permanent move to England to be with her boyfriend and dance as a principal ballerina with the Westminster Ballet. These days, Clara was always busy. If she wasn't dancing, she was teaching classes at the Westminster Ballet's Upper School. Amanda sorely missed her.

For the time being, Eddie was as close as she could get to a second bestie. She thought about how he always took the time to chat with her, regardless of the time of day. He was light-ning quick at replying to text messages too.

When was the last time she'd spoken to Clara? Had it been a month? She'd lost track of time. In a way she felt guilty, but knew once she got a hold of her friend, it would be as if they had never been apart.

When Eddie left, who would be around to hang out with? She enjoyed having a friend to care for. A twinge of sadness filled her.

Eddie's come and gone a handful of times. Why is this time any different? Is it because I know when he joins the army, I won't see him for a while? That without Clara, I don't really have any friends left around here?

She couldn't dwell on these thoughts. There was nothing she could do about Eddie or Clara. They had their own lives. Nothing stayed the same forever. Eventually, she'd move on to something bigger and better too. Or at least that's what she told herself.

Her mind moved to her home away from work, Disneyland. It held many happy memories for her. She wasn't about to let Eddie go home to London without experiencing why she enjoyed it so much.

Chapter Six

EDDIE

Eddie and the blokes hit the gym in Amanda's apartment complex hard and were back, dressed, and showered by four-thirty.

I need to get used to these early morning calls. David is always warning me that the military life means rising before the sun.

He wondered what time Collins had fallen asleep. Hadn't she still been awake when they went to bed at about ten? What time had she woken up to take care of him and the team?

Collins is like the Energizer bunny, always on the go with that multimillion-pound smile on her face.

The lads kept their conversations low as they finished their second breakfast.

There has to be a way I can show Collins how much I appreciate all of the extra effort she puts into make my trips to America special. Telling her I'm thankful isn't enough. I need to show her. Is there a way I can do that at Disneyland?

"Charlie, do you know what Collins has planned for today?" he asked the second-in-command officer on his team.

"Mum's the word, sir. She swore us to secrecy," he said, straight-faced.

"But you work for me! Come on, that isn't fair," Eddie protested.

"That may be true, sir, but you didn't go to the trouble of specially preparing all our meals." Charlie smirked and left the room to touch base with Jonathan.

I should've known my team could be bribed with some home-made food.

"There, all done," Amanda's neighbor, a Hollywood makeup artist, said as she set down her contouring brush.

"I should've known when Collins said I'd be playing a tourist today, she meant it literally."

He examined himself in the mirror. His normally sandy-blond hair was hidden by a vibrant red wig, with ends long enough to be secured into a short man bun. As he focused on his eyes, he noticed the colored contacts, which made them appeared brown. Cleverly applied makeup had added well-placed acne scars, completing the transformation. It was nothing short of astonishing.

"You did a bang-up job."

Amanda's neighbor grinned. "I did, didn't I?"

"Knock, knock, Eddie…" Amanda called out, poking her head around the bathroom door. "Oh, I'm sorry. I thought Princey was in here." She turned to leave, then took a step backward and frowned. Her gaze shifted between him and the hallway. "Are you a new member of the security team for today?"

Eddie's stomach muscles clenched as he tried to keep a straight face. He fought back laughter, tears welling up in his eyes. "It's… me…" he wheezed out between bursts of laughter. The shock and disbelief in her expression were priceless.

"Wow. I'm not usually so easily impressed, but man. You look like a whole new dude." Amanda examined him from all angles. "Nicely done, Angela." She high fived her neighbor.

Chapter Seven

AMANDA

The drive to Anaheim proceeded seamlessly as Amanda expertly directed the car through the side streets of Costa Mesa, Irvine, Tustin, Santa Ana, and Orange to avoid the freeway traffic. It was nearing seven-thirty in the morning.

Eddie was going to be upset with her once he learned about the amount of walking they'd be doing around the theme park. But in all honesty, she didn't feel too bad. She'd warned him to keep his workout light. *He* was the one who had chosen to run four miles this morning.

She glanced to her left, watching Eddie rest his head against the window.

He can sleep anywhere.

As tempted as she was to wake him, she decided to let him rest until they parked. It was going to be a long day.

I hope he enjoys his first trip to Disneyland. For me, it's the one place where nothing bad can happen. A place where I can just forget about what's going on in the real world.

Looking out at the passing scenery, she wondered when her own life had transformed into a living fairy tale. Never in a million years did she think she would be so content. She hummed "A Dream is a Wish Your Heart Makes" softly to herself.

As soon as the car pulled to a stop inside the parking structure, she bounced up and down in her seat. "We're here!" she shrieked.

Eddie yawned and stretched. "I'll admit, the car park is impressive. These Disney cast members understand how to park cars quickly and efficiently."

Of everything to be impressed by, Eddie chooses the parking structure? No way am I letting this be his top memory of the day.

Amanda spoke a mile a minute. "Wait until we get inside. I've got it all planned out. We'll start in Adventureland with the Haunted Mansion and work our way through everything I've highlighted on your maps based on the average standby waiting times. Our first Fastpass is going to be for Indiana Jones."

Eddie could only stare in disbelief.

Her enthusiasm rang through in her tone. "By the afternoon, the lines for a lot of the more popular attractions will be too long. You guys will be tired, so we'll use that time to slow down our pace and hit up Fantasyland."

Amanda paused to see if the security team had any questions. Her attempt at not overwhelming them was working so far. Only Jonathan had been privy to a glimpse at her intense level of preparation.

"You're speaking a foreign language, Collins. I have no idea what any of that means," Eddie joked. As Amanda handed each PPO a map and schedule, he unfolded his. "You've even scheduled our loo breaks? I'll just trust you on this, Collins. Lead away."

It was exactly as Amanda had hoped for.

Chapter Eight

EDDIE

As it finally began to sink in just where they were, Eddie's excitement level reverted to that of a child. It was actually happening—he was at Disneyland!

"You guys can stop me if I get too carried away. I'm just so excited." Amanda gave him puppy-dog eyes. "Oh, here are your 'First Visit' buttons. I got them ahead of time. Do you and the guys have any problems with wearing them?"

Eddie couldn't help but laugh. Nobody in the group could say no to Collins. She had them wrapped around her finger. Take this morning for instance: His girl had talked them into wearing matching Union Jack mouse-shaped silhouette shirts that said "Family Reunion."

At first, he'd had been rather reluctant to wear his; however, the more he saw other groups and families around him, the more he enjoyed the novelty of being immersed in the experience.

"Perfect. Now y'all need some ears."

Reaching inside her black-and-white backpack, Amanda retrieved six pairs of mouse ears and distributed them to the group. The lads reluctantly donned them. Eddie grinned even wider.

Amanda motioned for the group to huddle together closely in front of a mouse-shaped topiary. Reaching out her arm as far as she could, she said, "This is our first selfie of the day. Say 'Disney!'"

"Disney," everyone chimed in.

"Just a second," she said, zooming in on her phone to check the image.

"Do you want in on the betting pool?" Jonathan murmured into Eddie's ear. "Charlie has Ms. Collins's total number of photos ending up at about a hundred. I wager she'll be closer to five hundred."

"Don't put me down for an exact number. I'll wager she ends up running out of memory on her mobile."

"Yes, sir."

"Okay, I got it," Amanda said. They started for the escalator. "Oh, I almost forgot, there's a couple more topiaries by the tram stop and at the entrance to Downtown Disney we can get some cute selfies with."

I am so winning this bet.

Eddie fell in step with Jonathan. "If Charlie tries to up his number, don't let him."

"He's already tried," Jon chuckled.

"What did he bet?"

"Fifty quid."

"That's not too bad," Eddie mused. "What about you?"

"The same."

Confident nobody would touch him, he offered, "Put me down for a grand."

"You're certain?"

They watched Amanda take two more photos of the group lined up on the escalator.

"On second thought, double it."

~

Amanda highlighted a few points of interest as they walked from the tram drop-off location across from the World of Disney shop, past the ticket booths, to the main esplanade between Disneyland Park and Disney's California Adventure Park.

She sported her own rhinestone-covered mouse ears, over-sized white gloves, and a vibrant vintage-inspired turquoise dress that contrasted violently with her curly red hair. His girl bestie—a term she insisted on using that was growing on him —was never afraid to make a statement.

"So, this area used to be the main parking lot until 2001. Now it links the bus and shuttle stops and the Downtown Disney shopping district. We're heading to Disneyland Park today. Trying to do California Adventure, too, would be overkill. I'm ambitious, but even I know the limits of what's enjoyable." Amanda chuckled.

Eddie's anticipation of taking his first steps on Main Street was reaching a peak. The group queued up behind one of the many turnstiles to have their digital tickets scanned from Amanda's mobile. He glanced around, taking in the scene.

There were so many people, but they all had two things in common—one, each person had a goofy grin on their face, and two, they were all outfitted in Disney-themed attire. The buzz of excitement among the crowd grew, everyone eager for Disneyland to officially open.

It was a slightly chilly Southern California morning, the dampness of the night still lingering in the air. Surprisingly, very few people had any sweaters or jackets with them.

Eddie was caught off guard as a train horn sounded, then passed overhead. "What was that?" he asked, pointing up.

Amanda turned and squinted up toward the sun. "Oh, that's the Monorail. It's an attraction that runs from Tomorrowland to the Downtown Disney station and back. I have us scheduled to enjoy that before dinner at the Napa Rose inside the Grand Californian Hotel and Spa."

Eddie absorbed the information as he observed the floral displays cleverly arranged to form a giant mouse head just past the iron gates at the entrance. The background music grew louder and transitioned into a catchy melody of tunes from classic animated Disney films.

At fifteen minutes to eight, the queue finally began to move. The crowds slowly shuffled toward Main Street. Amanda stopped them for yet another group selfie in front of the floral display, then directed them to the left side of Main Street under the railroad station bridge.

Eddie's senses were on overload. The catchy music, the scent of cinnamon churros, and colorful window displays made him wish he could freeze time just so he could stop and examine every single detail that caught his attention. "Is that a horse and a streetcar? And a firehouse? Why is everyone bottlenecked here?"

They passed the flagpole and stood across from the Coke sign at the tail end of Main Street. Amanda raised her voice to be heard over the crowd. "We have to wait here until they pull the rope away for us to officially enter the park. They always let their guests in about fifteen minutes before opening to shop for souvenirs. We can try to move closer to the front, but it's not worth it. As soon as the welcome announcement plays, we're going to the end of Main Street and to the left to Adventureland. We'll come back to the castle, Partners Statue, and main hub to the park after we get the first few rides knocked out."

Eddie nodded, not entirely sure about all the places she'd mentioned. His security team moved in closer out of habit, eyes scanning their surroundings to ensure safety. His gaze lingered on the piano just outside the Coke corner. He pictured himself playing a tune for Amanda as she sat right next to him, singing loudly and off-key.

The voice of the public-address speaker suddenly boomed out, "Ladies and gentleman, boys and girls, welcome to Disneyland." The crowd cheered. The announcement politely requested that everyone walk, not run, to their destination.

Eddie shivered in delight. He resisted the urge to pinch himself to see if he really was here.

A team of three cast members greeted the crowd with smiles. "All right, everyone, welcome to Disneyland! We're going to slowly pull back the rope. Please walk and be mindful of others around you. Have a magical day." Surprisingly, the visitors listened to their instructions.

Amanda gently held Eddie's hand. Hers was warm and so small. An electric spark of energy bounded through his body.

"Here we go. Power walk to the left and straight on 'til you see the Haunted Mansion," she announced to the group. "Trust me, you'll know it when you see it. If for some reason we get separated, call my cell number. It's on the top of every-body's map and schedule for the day. The meet-up location is marked on each map."

Eddie matched Amanda's pace. Already, he could tell they would do a fair bit of walking. The muscles in his legs ached. Why had he insisted on working out today? He should've listened to Collins.

They passed under a wooden tiki-themed sign indicating the entrance to Adventureland. Amanda slowed her pace. "On your left, you'll notice the Enchanted Tiki Room. They have the world's best pineapple soft serve. It's Clara's favorite thing at the park. We'll come back here later for the Jungle Cruise, Indiana Jones, and Pirates of the Caribbean."

This part of the theme park felt distinctly different from Main Street. Thick trees and soft animal sounds created the ambiance of a forest. Was it more humid too? The pathway opened up to reveal a large body of water. Steam billowed out of the smokestacks of an early twentieth-century riverboat. He read the name of the boat on the side—Mark Twain. "Brilliant."

Jonathan wasn't easily impressed, but Eddie could tell he was finding it hard to mask his own excitement. His eyes darted around just as Eddie's did. They arrived at the large antebellum-style home. Walking through the steel gates, he saw the line for the attraction wove through a graveyard and past a horseless carriage.

Amanda's eyes sparkled with mirth. "So this is the original Haunted Mansion. Each Disney Park around the world has their own version. Pretty awesome, isn't it?"

Eddie had no idea what to expect. Was this a dark ride? Were they just going to walk through the home? When it was finally their turn to go inside, he was surprised to find they stood in a wood-paneled hallway.

Haunting music played in the background. The air-conditioning was on full blast, creating a cold and otherworldly environment. Eddie's eyes took a few moments to adjust to the dim lighting inside. The walls suddenly slid open, revealing a doorless chamber.

"Welcome, foolish mortals," a cast member in a butler costume deadpanned. "Kindly enter the chamber and drag your bodies to the dead center of the room."

Eddie sniggered. The doors shut and the room darkened. The floor jolted. Was it moving? A dark and disembodied voice came over the speaker. Were the paintings on the wall stretching? He felt the floor come to a halt.

Suddenly, a clap of thunder sent the lights out. A lifeless body suspended from the ceiling, then vanished. A voice screamed and the doors slid open. Eddie jumped. His nerves were slightly on edge. They walked down a dim hallway, where paintings flashed, revealing a normal image, then a skeletal image. The bust forms at the end of the hall followed his gaze no matter where he looked.

Amanda tugged his hand. Eddie was grateful for the distraction from the eerie atmosphere. Otherwise, he might have remained staring at the busts. Black buggies awaited them ahead.

"We can ride two by two. I call Princey," Amanda said, leading them to the front of the line. They hopped in as the pull bar came down and were whisked away through the attraction.

Amanda scooted closer to Eddie. He caught a whiff of her lavender and citrus fragrance. The stiff cotton of her dress's skirt brushed lightly against his leg. He bit the inside of his cheek, resisting the urge to wrap his arms around her and instead gripping the pull bar, his knuckles turning white.

Luckily, this was a dark ride. Amanda shouldn't be able to see his discomfort. Could he last all day fighting the obvious feelings that were unmistakably growing inside of him? Was it the atmosphere of being at Disneyland? He gulped.

At this rate, I'll be telling Collins how much I like her before we finish the ride. But what if she doesn't see me the same way that I see her? I can't let her find out now and risk ruining the day. I'll have to keep my distance from her. Yeah, that's what I'll do. If I'm not near her, maybe, just maybe, I'll be able to keep myself in check.

Chapter Nine

AMANDA

"You could have warned us Splash Mountain would cause us to get sodding wet," one of the protection officers grumbled to the group, shaking his hands to get the excess water off.

Jonathan burst into laughter, the driest member of the group. "What did you expect would happen based on the name Splash Mountain? Didn't you read any of the signs leading up to the loading area?"

Eddie crossed his arms and looked the PPO over. "That's what you get for being on your mobile the entire time we were queued up. Be thankful Collins passed you a plastic bag to keep it dry."

Amanda sensed the guys were getting hungry. Hanger never looked well on anyone. She glanced at her watch—it was twelve-thirty, perfect. They had just enough time to make their way over to the Blue Bayou for their lunch reservation.

Clapping her hands together, she caught the group's attention. They all turned their focus to her, awaiting further instructions. "Okay, kiddos. Loo break, then lunch. Lunch is indoors. We have to be over there in ten minutes. I'll wait here for you guys."

Amanda parked herself on a vacant bench next to the stroller-parking area between Splash Mountain and a character meet and greet. She enjoyed seeing the joy on the little faces of the children as they interacted with the characters and hearing them ask for autographs. Glancing toward the nearby gift shop, a window that looked into a kitchen revealed a cast member dipping a crisp apple into a pot of gooey, hot caramel.

Eddie and the team broke away. She was alone for the first time that day. So far, aside from being stuck on the Indiana Jones attraction, everything was moving along swimmingly. She let out a sigh, feeling the ache of her feet.

Looking at her swollen ankles and strappy sandals, she had no one to blame but herself. She'd known they'd be doing a lot of walking and had still opted to look cute instead of being practical. Was she trying to impress Eddie? The answer was obvious… of course. She knew she was going to have blisters upon blisters by the end of the day. Monday was going to be long when she worked the seven-hour flight to Toronto.

Amanda's thoughts shifted to Eddie. Was he truly enjoying himself, or was he disappointed? She hadn't seen the excited reaction she expected out of him. If anything, Eddie didn't even act as if he wanted to be in her vicinity. How many attempts had she made to sit next to him?

I thought we were on the road to something deeper. Was I wrong?

Amanda put on her game face. She was committed to keeping everyone going strong. Eddie and the team returned, and they walked over to the Blue Bayou Restaurant. She walked alongside Jonathan, asking him how they'd enjoyed the day so far.

His eyes crinkled. "I'd say right now it's a roaring success. Just keep the mates fed, and we'll be a whole new bunch."

Amanda hoped that was the case as she checked in with the hostess. They were shown to a table right on the waterline. Eddie claimed the seat closest to the water's edge. She sat at the head of the table, three seats away from Eddie, whose eyes kept watching the boats from the Pirates of the Caribbean pass by. There was a faint scent of chlorine and the sound of soft banjo music.

"Everything on the menu is delicious, but stay clear of the Monte Cristo," she warned them. "It's really rich and might give you stomach problems later."

Eddie nodded and reviewed the other options. "Didn't you say the mint julep is refreshing?"

He was paying attention to me after all on the train ride around the park when I talked about the mint juleps and beignets.

As they waited for lunch, the group engaged in conversation and bantered. "What's been everybody's favorite attraction so far?" Amanda asked.

Space Mountain in Tomorrowland received two votes, Jonathan selected Star Tours—receiving a high five from her—and the last two votes went to Finding Nemo and Eddie's favorite, the Jungle Cruise.

He began spouting bad puns. "I'm sure after lunch, wherever we may be headed is going to be fun. I'm not taking it for granite."

Jonathan and the guys groaned. Amanda had to hand it to Eddie. He was a quick study when it came to using the Jungle Cruise skipper's jokes. She always enjoyed the beheading pun when they passed the Trader Sam statue at the end of the ride, and the joke about the wall being taken for granite instead of stone.

The mood shifted as soon as the food arrived at the table. Despite her warning, most of the group had decided to order the Monte Cristo. They shoveled down their food. Amanda carefully cut into her own roasted chicken. She stared at the light-up ice cube in her drink. Should she mention the Alice teacups were next? No, it could be a fun surprise.

She caught Eddie staring at her between bites. He was making her feel almost self-conscious. He really wasn't subtle. She still wasn't used to seeing him in his disguise.

She cleared her throat. "From now to parade time, we'll cover Fantasyland, Toontown and It's a Small World. You can nap on Small World if you want, but it's one of the must-see and dos here. Even if you don't enjoy it, the art inside alone is ammmmmmmaaaazing. Mary Blair, the artist who did a lot of the work on *Peter Pan* and *Alice*, designed most of it. Actually, it was used at one of the world's fairs."

"I want to sit in the front row, if that can be arranged," Eddie said quietly.

"We won't get wet on it, will we?" one of the protection officers asked.

Chapter Ten

EDDIE

After dessert, Amanda moved to pay for their meal despite Eddie's protests. Their server returned and discreetly asked if she could speak to Amanda. She put her napkin down, stood from her chair, and stepped to the side.

Eddie's eyes lingered on her. He watched her face as she wrinkled her nose and pouted her lips. They were full and a vibrant red. He'd envisioned kissing those lips so many times. Her cheeks grew a delightful rosy color. As she returned to the table, she huffed, and then riffled through her wallet.

"Everything all right?" he asked with concern.

Amanda didn't meet his eyes. "Fine." Her answer was clipped. She passed another credit card to the server. "Try this one." She sat back down and blew her flyaway hairs out of her face.

Eddie didn't want to draw too much attention to her in case she needed a moment to compose herself. "Hey, blokes, you may want to use the loo here. Our next scheduled break isn't for a while," he pointed out.

"Good point, sir." Jonathan gave him a knowing look. He

and Eddie remained behind while everyone else gave them some space.

The server returned again. "I'm sorry, but this card was declined as well."

Amanda's face was now bright red. "I don't understand. I just checked it this morning. I should have a zero balance."

Eddie jumped in. "Is there a problem with the bill?"

Amanda's shoulders hunched in defeat. "My debit and credit cards were both declined," she mumbled.

Eddie could see how embarrassing that might be to a proud and confident woman like Amanda. He felt his back pocket for his own wallet. "Here." He took out a silver chrome bank card, passing it to the server. "This should do the trick."

"Can I see some photo ID, please?" the server asked. Eddie hesitated. His fingers lingered over his wallet as he passed his driver's license over.

Amanda's face whitened. "No. You shouldn't do that."

The server looked at the photo on the card and back to Eddie several times. "I'm afraid we can't accept this. This photo doesn't match your face or the name on the card."

He frowned. The name on the card should have said Edmund Wales. Where was the problem? His eyes grew wide. The ID said Prince Edmund and had his normal appearance on it. He looked nothing like his photo.

Jonathan took out his own wallet. "Use this card and photo ID. If that doesn't work, I have the cash." The server managed a tight smile and made a third attempt to process a payment card.

Eddie and Amanda glanced at Jonathan, who appeared unfazed. "The palace can reimburse me." He chuckled. "Is this the first time you've been asked for a photo ID and had your card refused, sir?"

Eddie laughed to himself. "It is."

Amanda recovered from her initial shock as she scrolled

through the banking app on her phone. "I still don't get it. This says I don't owe anything—" She paused. "Oh… the payment is still pending." Relief washed over her face as she closed the app and stowed her phone away.

The server brought back the approved slip for a signature as the team returned to the table, blissfully unaware of the earlier chaos. Eddie was saved from having to say anything to Amanda. Her mouth opened and closed.

Can I guess it was to tell me off for trying to pay?

Chapter Eleven

AMANDA

"I'm so tired!" Amanda exclaimed. The afternoon had been jam-packed with a parade viewing and powering through almost every single attraction in Fantasyland, Toontown, and Tomorrowland. It was eight at night. The group sat on the cold cement, camped in the front area of the Rivers of America, awaiting the start of the nighttime entertainment as the wind picked up.

She yawned again. "I could really go for some hot chocolate right about now, but I don't wanna get up and lose our spot."

It's too late for coffee and Disney hot chocolate is extra sweet. It would be the perfect pick-me-up. I'm so cozy though with Eddie's arms around me. Can I trust one of the guys to get one for me? She looked at Eddie. *No, I can't. That's taking them away from their job. Princey's safety is the most important priority. I guess I'll just get it myself.*

Just as she was about to rise and stumble through the sea of people behind her, a cast member in a red-and-blue plaid Guest Relations uniform tapped her on the shoulder. "I'm so sorry to bother you, but are you Amanda Collins?"

She froze. *Am I in trouble? He knows my name. What did I do?*

"Yes?" she said hesitantly.

The man nodded. "Great. If you and your party would please follow me. We have your evening accommodations ready for you."

Her mouth opened and closed. What exactly did he mean? Eddie shrugged. Jon's expression was blank. Her attention was redirected to the cast member. "Um … sure … sounds good."

Weaving through the crowd of families waiting for the show, and the sea of strollers, the cast member guided them toward the bridge above the Rivers of America, and the gate near the treehouse.

Amanda's pulse beat rapidly. Her breath hitched. "No way!" she exclaimed, knowing *exactly* where they were being taken.

The cast member grinned and nodded in confirmation as they ascended the steps above the Pirates of the Caribbean. He opened the door. "This has been reserved this evening on your behalf."

Inside the room, the walls were a soft cream hue, and were adorned with framed photos of the German castle Neuschwanstein, captured from varying angles. Opposite the photos was a stately grandfather clock, its silhouette depicting Cinderella dancing with her prince. A mahogany coffee table, a blue-and-gold velvet sofa, and two wingback chairs comprised the modest furniture.

A faux fire radiated warmth throughout the room. Above the fireplace, LED lights shaped like fireworks shimmered, resembling thousands of fairy lights. Amanda was certain they would discover other peculiar trinkets and treasures that held special meaning to Walt Disney himself.

"Oh. My. Gosh. This is really happening! The Dream Suite," she squealed, and instantly started darting around the room, snapping photo after photo and selfie after selfie, much to the amusement of those around her. Experiencing the inside of the Dream Suite was on her bucket list, but never once had she thought it could actually happen.

Eddie wore a cheesy grin on his face.

Chapter Twelve

EDDIE

"Sir, I think the plan was a huge success." Jonathan discreetly thanked the cast member, who saw himself out and closed the door behind him.

Eddie couldn't believe he had managed to pull off the surprise and stun Amanda. Her smile was electric. She reminded him of one of the dolls from inside It's a Small World. He'd never seen her so excited.

"Eddie? You did this?" Amanda exclaimed. He nodded. She launched herself at him and hugged him tightly. "Thank you, thank you, thank you, thank you."

She melted into his arms. He allowed himself to savor the embrace, making no effort to move, holding her close. His Adam's apple bobbed up and down as he was caught in a whirlwind of emotions, leaving him momentarily speechless. Blood rushed to his ears, turning them bright red.

Amanda's hair was tangled in loose, frizzy waves around her face, freed from the confines of her mouse-shaped head-band. He gazed into her green eyes. All the doubts from earlier vanished. If being Amanda's bestie felt this extraordinary, he could only imagine what it would be like to be her boyfriend.

He leaned in and kissed her softly and tenderly, captivated by her intoxicating scent of chocolate and cinnamon and the emotions of pure joy emanating from her. Her lips were like velvet, smooth and soft.

Suddenly, she froze and pulled back, leaving the lingering warmth from the unexpected kiss.

"But I thought you were upset with me," she sputtered.

"Is that what you've been thinking all day, Collins? Why would I be upset with you?" Eddie's stomach twisted in knots. "I've been trying to keep my distance all day to control myself around you. I like you. A lot. I find you incredibly attractive."

Amanda took two steps back. "Are you being serious right now?" She placed her hands on top of her head. "I swear, from the vibe you've been giving me all day, I thought you were disappointed and having a lousy time."

Eddie reached up, hesitating before he lowered his hand, remembering not to mess with the wig. "Amanda, I'm always blown away by everything you do for me. For the team. But this trip, you've gone to infinity and beyond. Today has been one of the best days of my life. The Dream Suite was just one small way of my being able to give back to you and say thank you."

"Wow, just wow." Amanda staggered and sank onto the antique blue-and-gold velvet couch. "Nice *Toy Story* reference by the way."

"Thanks."

Jonathan cleared his throat. He had a knack for reappearing at inopportune times, and Eddie wished he'd stay away a little bit longer. "I'm sorry to interrupt, but I just wanted to let you two know that showtime is five minutes away."

"Thanks, Jon." Eddie nodded. He stepped over to Amanda, gently taking her hand and leading her over to the balcony, where they would watch the show. "We can discuss this after. We obviously have a lot to clear up. I don't want you to miss the show, especially since apparently, this is one of the best viewing areas in the entire theme park."

~

At midnight, Disneyland was closing. They'd stayed as long as they dared.

Strolling past the castle, Eddie chuckled. "Honestly, this is so much cleaner and more beautifully lit than anything my family owns."

Amanda seemed momentarily taken aback by his comment. "Sometimes I forget just who you are, Princey."

They took in the soft display of pink and blue lights on the castle and the popcorn lights illuminating Main Street as one of the last sets of people within the theme park. This truly was one of the most magical and happiest places on Earth.

On the ride back to her apartment, the car was cloaked in silence. The members of the protection team were fast asleep, except for Jonathon, who was driving. Eddie's mind was consumed by thoughts of when he would have another opportunity like this to spend time with Amanda.

He laced his fingers through hers. In a soft voice, he began, "Collins, until tonight, I wasn't exactly sure how you felt about me. You're my girl and, as you might say, one of my besties." He tensed all the muscles in his body. "But I want more. Would you… uh… that is… what do you think about us taking things to the next level?"

Amanda turned her body toward Eddie, her breathing increasing. She bit her lip and brushed her hair out of her face, her eyes glistening with a hint of tears. "If you're asking if I'd be open to dating you, I'd like that. As I've told you before, I've *always* had a crush on you. You're my literal dream come true."

"That makes me like you even more."

Amanda sighed, but it was a happy sound. "The last couple of months, I feel like things have changed between us. You're not just the cousin of my best friend's boyfriend. You're *my* friend. You're one of my besties too. This feels like the natural next step."

Eddie reached for her hand and, as soft as a butterfly's wing, placed a kiss on it. In the rearview mirror, Jonathan's eyes met his. His protection officer winked and returned his eyes to the road.

I don't think I can be much happier than I am now. With my girl right beside me, all is right in the world. She's my princess charming.

Chapter Thirteen

EDDIE

Morning came all too quickly. With his backpack slung over one shoulder, Eddie turned and spied a pajama-clad Amanda standing in the doorway. "I can't believe how early you got up for this."

She smiled, her eyes a little tired but still sparkling like vibrant emeralds. "I wouldn't miss saying goodbye to my favorite person."

He pulled her into a warm embrace, savoring the feeling of holding his girlfriend in his arms. That had to be the most beautiful word in the English language. "You know, I've had an incredible visit. I just wish it didn't have to end."

"Me too," Amanda whispered, her voice tinged with sadness. "All good things have to end eventually, and you know, the sooner you leave, the faster you can return."

He nodded, pressing a tender kiss to her forehead. The curly wisps that had escaped her braid tickled his nose. "You have it backward, Collins—you mean the sooner you can come to London."

"Right you are, Princey." They stood there for a moment,

lost in each other's eyes, the reality of the impending separation heavy in the air.

He squeezed her hand. "I'll text or ring you when I can. It's going to be a little sporadic once I enter basic training."

"Sporadic messages are better than nothing," Amanda agreed, her voice steadier now. "Have a safe trip home."

"I will." He leaned in and kissed her softly, savoring the taste and the touch one last time before he reluctantly let go. "Bye, Collins."

"Bye, Princey."

He climbed into the car and watched Amanda reenter her apartment. He felt reluctant to leave Southern California, and in particular Amanda, behind. The goodbyes were always like a punch to the gut. Being able to speak over video chat wouldn't be the same as seeing his brilliant girlfriend in person.

Shifting his backpack from the seat to the ground, he noticed it was considerably heavier than it had been several minutes before. He unzipped the larger of the two compartments to rearrange the contents. His hands froze as he stared in disbelief at encountering five care packages. Amanda must have put them together for everyone for their flight home.

How and when did she manage to sneak these in? There's something there for each bloke on my team. Amanda, you are unbelievable.

Once inside their chartered plane, Eddie distributed the packages. Each one was carefully and thoughtfully tailored to the individual and wrapped in white tissue paper with little mouse heads. They contained cookies, candies, keychains, and a few other souvenir goodies.

The cornerstone of everyone's package, however, was the group photo of his entire team had taken in Toontown when meeting the boss mouse for the first time. The guys never smiled much, but in this case, they had made an exception.

His hands brushed the corner of the frame. Eddie stared at the photo. Grinning from ear to ear, Amanda stood in the center, beaming proudly amidst the group with her arms wrapped around the boss mouse. He hugged the photo to his chest. There really was no person like Amanda.

All his PPOs had fallen in love with her too. Would the same hold true when it came time to meet his family? He worried, especially at the thought of his mother, Queen Agnus, meeting Amanda. Mum was highly traditional compared to the more moderate views held by his father. She had only just begun to relent on her disapproval at the idea of having an American enter the family with Clara now engaged to David.

If anyone can hold their own with Mum, Amanda can.

For the first time in his life, Eddie wondered if Amanda could be the one. The realization struck him like a bolt of lightning. It was a stark departure from the flings he'd had with his previous set of girlfriends. She was different in every sense of the word.

He was drawn to her wit, her charm, her sass, and her pizazz. She challenged him in ways he had never been pushed before. Her presence in his life encouraged growth, exploration, and breaking free from his comfort zones. He admired her for that, how she didn't hesitate to speak her mind and encourage him to be the best version of himself.

There was even a moment when Amanda had poked fun at him for being lazy. "You have no hobbies," she'd said. "You need to discover what you like and don't like. You won't have any idea about that until you venture out into the world and have some adventures. With me as your guide, you're sure to take a few wrong turns, but that's part of the journey."

It made him laugh, but it also made him reflect. He respected her for being candid, for keeping him on his toes. Amanda had seamlessly become an integral part of his world. The pull she had on his heart continued to grow stronger with each passing day.

As the plane crossed over the heart of the United States, Eddie's focus gravitated to his philanthropic work. Being able to collaborate with David on their joint venture, the Wales and Leeds Trust, shortened to Waleeds, was the part of being a royal he was growing to love the most. He was still only beginning to understand the significant impact he could make on the lives of the people they aimed to assist.

Spreading out the printed emails from David, Eddie began to read through, highlight, and annotate his thoughts on a variety of topics. Despite the ease of digital access, his cousin preferred having a physical copy of all their communications.

Eddie was particularly proud of his fundraising ideas for the next financial quarter. As the Prince of Wales, he had access to the farm on the Duchy of Cornwall property. The land yielded many crops that could be sold at the market. Honey, jams, organic fresh fruits—all things he didn't need, but could be so helpful to others. The proceeds from those sales could go to Waleeds. He knew he needed to do more research to figure out all the details, but one question remained—would David approve?

Five months ago, he'd hit an all-time low after his reckless behavior had caused Clara to break her foot. That could have ended her career. He'd never felt more ashamed of himself. Despite all the things Clara could have done, she had chosen to be a bigger person and forgive him.

More recently, she had taken him under her wing and

adopted him as a younger brother. He had grown to respect and depend upon her. Eddie had already learned a lot of valuable lessons.

The kindness she's shown me has made me want to be a better brother to my own sister, Alice.

Chapter Fourteen

EDDIE

Dear Amanda,

I hope you aren't angry that I've gone silent the last six weeks. I promise that it wasn't intentional. Believe it or not, I wasn't allowed to write to you. Letter writing and being able to have any contact with our loved ones is a privilege that isn't earned until basic training is nearly over.

I won't bore you with the details, but I will say that I've been mentally and physically exhausted in every possible way the last couple of weeks. They've managed to rip us to bits, then build us back up. I'm a different person, and yet, I'm also still Eddie. I'm not sure how to properly describe it. I hope you'll recognize me when this is all over.

Sometimes at night, I dream about you and Disneyland. It's hard to believe it was only a few short weeks ago. I can't wait until I can see you on video chat again, or better yet, maybe you'll consider coming to my passing out ceremony.

Yours,
Eddie

Chapter Fifteen

AMANDA

Dear Eddie,

I squealed so loudly when I opened my mailbox and saw I had a letter from across the pond, and from you, nonetheless. I figured that if you weren't kidnapped by a band of ninjas, there had to be a good reason I hadn't heard from you.

It's just weird they'd want you to keep from outside contact for so long, but I understand. My dad was in the military. We were both wrong when we thought we'd be able to chat weekly.

I've been in contact with David, and he's given me the lowdown of what you've probably been going through. I don't envy you one bit. All I can say is, don't worry about me. I can take care of myself and I'm not going anywhere. I'm a Collins. We're hard to get rid of.

I'm counting down until your basic training days are over too! Being cut off from you has been difficult and I have the date of your graduation circled on the calendar. I'm going to do my best to make it to the UK to see you graduate.

Yours,
Amanda

Chapter Sixteen

EDDIE

Dear Amanda,

I know you tried your best to make it to graduation and you can't control the weather. The hurricane caught everybody off guard. It was raining rugby-ball-sized hail when the platoon stepped out onto the parade ground, but you know the army... rain or shine, we carry on. They'd never let "a little rain" ruin our parade. Literally.

Father was there and it was great to see him so happy, but still I'd rather you were there instead of him. Clara played the video for me to see. It brought a big smile to my face. You're even more gorgeous than I remember. I only wish your mobile had been turned on so we could've spoken in person... which brings me to the reason you're getting snail mail.

I'm not sure if you received the text I sent you this afternoon, but just in case, I'd tell you that right after the ceremony, Father caught me off guard. He announced to me and the family that he'd gotten me placed in the first available army riding course. He wants me to graduate and on ceremonial duty "without undue delay."

I was so angry. He could've at least spoken to me beforehand! As soon as I cleared out of the basic training barracks, I was ordered to report directly to the Windsor Riding School. There was no downtime, and sadly, now I have at least another three weeks before we can talk again.

I'm sorry. I hope you understand.

Yours,

Eddie

Chapter Seventeen

AMANDA

Dear Eddie,

Okay, this time I may have cried a little.
I was driving home from BBQ Shack when the
text came through. I didn't see it in time. When
I called you, your phone went right to voicemail.
When I got home, I had an overnight express
envelope with your letter in it, then I touched
base with David and Clara. They were pretty
upset with your dad too.

Three more weeks? *Groans* I can do it.
You can do it. I mean, we don't have much of
a choice. Do we? The king is not just your dad,
but also the head of the military and your
commanding officer. You kind of have to do
what he says. As a son and a soldier. As
much as it sucks, it is what it is. I accept it.

As frustrated as we both are, I'm sure his heart is in the right place.

I know you love horses and riding and that this next part of your training should hopefully be more enjoyable than basic was. When you get your address, let me know what it is so I can send you some more care packages. Counting down the days. Again.

Wait until I see you again. I have three new cookbooks of recipes I want to try out on you (and maybe the guys too).

Yours,
Amanda

Chapter Eighteen

EDDIE

The training school of the Household Cavalry Mounted Regiment was situated on the grounds of Windsor Castle. Entering the riding school compound two days later, Eddie marched in formation with some of the other members of his recruitment class.

They lined up, standing at attention, facing their horses and gripping the reins firmly. Outside, the rain pounded against the riding school's covered training area in droves. The smell of mud mixed with the scent of hay and horses.

The commanding officers strode into the riding school room for their first general inspection. Eddie swallowed nervously, feeling the moisture on his palms. He fought the urge to rub them against his trousers.

"When directed, you will call out your name and the name of the horse you are riding," the riding master, Corporal of Horse Andrew Reed, bellowed. He was the trainer for the next few months.

The atmosphere in the room shifted noticeably, the collective nervousness of the recruits palpable.

He doesn't look too dangerous. I hope.

Each recruit was dressed in the standard army-issue gear: a camo jacket, either a red or blue helmet, khaki trousers, and riding boots. The red helmet denoted the recruit belonged to the Life Guards division, of which Eddie was a member, while the blue indicated membership to the Blues and Royals.

In sequence, each recruit yelled out their name, moving down the line. Eddie rocked back and forth on his heels, and his horse stomped its hoof, sensing his agitation. Horses had a knack for picking up on human emotions. Finally, his turn came.

"Trooper Wales reporting for duty, riding Freddy, sir!" he bellowed, projecting his voice.

Freddy snorted, as if to say, "That's right. I'm important too. Don't forget it."

Eddie smirked at his mount. The commanding officers didn't blink at his introduction.

"Welcome, Trooper Wales. And just whereabouts are you from?" the officer questioned.

He'd never considered exactly where his home base was. It could be anywhere. "From London, sir," he replied, his voice more reserved. In a personal conversation, he needn't be so loud.

"Another city chap, huh? And a member of the Life Guards. Excellent. Be prepared for some hard work," the commanding officer commented, then moved on down the line, inspecting the other recruits.

The officer stood tall with his hands behind his back, carrying his riding crop. Eddie maintained a neutral expression. Despite the temptation to see how the others were handling the pressure, he kept his gaze firmly fixed on Freddy.

"Troopers at ease!" The recruits stomped their feet and turned to face the riding master. "Today you will mount your horse and learn to walk. Watch closely, as this demonstration will only be done once. Place your arms on the middle of the saddle and get a good firm jump off the ground. Place your body weight over your arms and push yourself up into position onto the horse."

The recruits stared at the riding master in bewilderment. They were expected to jump on? No mounting blocks? Eddie gulped. Was he strong enough to pull himself up?

The riding master broke the silence. "Get to it!" he exclaimed.

The recruits clambered to get to the sides of their horses, to the sound of heavy footfalls and the chains of the horses' bridles jingling. The men grunted and breathed hard. Eddie confidently took hold of his horse's reins.

How hard can this be?

He cockily placed his arms on the saddle and jumped, only to have his horse move away. He fell to the floor in a heap.

Oh, no you don't. Let's do this again, Freddy.

Eddie tried again, pushing hard off the ground, only to have his arms give out. He hadn't gripped the saddle in the right spot. He leaned over the horse, struggling to pull himself off, and was forced to jump down.

Glancing around the room, he noticed he wasn't the only one struggling. His training mates fell to the ground in an almost constant rhythm. A few jumped too hard, others too soft, or couldn't get their horses to behave.

His father often joked Eddie could ride before he could walk. Having grown up around horses all his life, he couldn't believe how different army-style riding was compared to that of normal riding. A military-issued saddle was much farther forward compared to his polo and riding saddles.

On his fifth attempt, Eddie jumped off the ground and shimmied his way to a place where he could get himself up. His muscles screamed in protest.

Already his shoulders and biceps felt as if he had gone four or five rounds of strength training with David. He took several deep breaths and leaned over to pat his horse. Freddy's eyes closed lazily as he snorted. Beads of perspiration ran down the sides of Eddie's face.

The riding master had a keen eye. "Trooper Wales, you're the first one to get onto your mount. Time to dismount and do it quicker."

Eddie groaned internally. "Yes, Corporal."

He swung his legs off and braced himself for the landing. His legs wobbled in protest and felt just as stiff as his arms. He took two steps forward to brace himself.

"Don't move those legs once they hit the ground," Corporal Reed commanded, surveying his recruits. "Use your legs to get a really good push off the ground. This is the easy part, boys. Welcome to the Household Cavalry." The riding master laughed sardonically.

It was a rude awakening. Many considered the Household Cavalry's sixteen-week riding course to be among the most difficult in the British Army. Recruits who had successfully survived and completed basic training often found themselves struggling to master horse riding within such a tight time frame.

Eddie was pleased to see some of his other recruits were getting on just as he had. They managed to swing themselves up and latch on to their horses, albeit not very gracefully—but that would come in time.

"Steady on! Troopers, once you have a seat on your mount, sit tall and wait for further instructions!" Now that almost all the recruits had succeeded in mounting their horses, they were given a brief reprieve to catch their breath.

Eddie's thoughts turned to the last few months. Had boot camp truly been only two months ago? He shivered at the painful memories. He understood that no matter what, there would be some shock, curiosity, and cold-shoulder treatment at being around a royal.

It was something both David and his father had hounded into him. As a royal, he needed to have thick skin. He would always have to work harder than anyone to prove himself. Hearing it and experiencing it, however, were two different matters.

How would the others treat him this time? Would they think he was a spoiled prick, as they did in basic training? Would they believe he couldn't handle the course again? The last two courses were barely survivable. Only the memories of his time with Amanda kept him motivated.

Corporal Reed's eagle eyes never missed any details. He rode his charger, a well-muscled and tall Irish black horse, reviewing his men. All the horses of the Household Cavalry were of a similar make, at a minimum of sixteen hands high. They could be fearsome horses. That was the theory, at least, in the days of Napoleon. The black was supposed to terrify England's enemies.

Corporal Reed drew out his next set of instructions. "All right, then, boys, time to take the horses for a little walk. Your job is to squeeze the horse with your legs and control its direction of movement with the reins. Your horse has more experience than you lot; they are the real masters of the school. Let them take on most of the work. Be firm, yet gentle."

They played follow the leader and took turns slowly attempting to have their horse walk around the covered circuit. Falling off or being "binned" became the theme of the day. The troopers took fall after fall, Eddie included. He groaned and looked up at his horse.

Could he stay on the ground and lie there? His body was stiff. He slowly moved to sit up; his legs quivered under him with overuse.

"Get up!" Corporal Reed yelled. Eddie had no choice and huffed as he clumsily mounted his horse again. A few sniggers from behind him did not go unnoticed by the riding master.

"You think this is right fun entertainment, do you? Let's see how you handle a slow trot." The group groaned. Corporal Reed was strict, but fair. He treated everyone the same.

The expected workload continually increased over the next few days. Everyone was always too tired at the end of the day to say much. They slept hard on uncomfortable twin-sized beds in the barracks opposite the barns.

Their duties appeared never-ending. Currently, Eddie found himself counting down the minutes until they were released to the commissary for lunch. Too bad it was only seven in the morning.

Corporal Reed ordered the recruits to assemble in formation. "This morning, you will take on the added responsibility of saddling your horses. By now, you should be aware of what all the major kit pieces are and have some idea of the process. Use your instincts. Is that understood?"

"Yes, Corporal." They saluted and scrambled to grab the horse tack from the equipment wall. They had no time for chatter. Eddie gritted his teeth as his tight arms took on the twelve kilos of required items.

The fact that the commanding officers had seen fit to leave the group alone to "figure things out" didn't seem proper. Eddie was positive this was a test to see if they could learn to work together from the start.

His fingers moved proficiently through the saddling process, having done his own saddling thousands of times. He made quick work of the drill and stood grooming his horse, speaking in soft tones to it. He peeked over to see how the other members of the group were performing.

In the stall next to him, the tallest member of his training class—"Too-Tall," as Eddie had heard others call him—was having a particularly difficult time. He stared with his large gray eyes at the saddle in contemplation, sticking his tongue out.

He was nearly six foot eight. As tall as Eddie was, he felt almost dwarfed next to Too-Tall. Should he offer to help? So far, Eddie had been treated as an outsider to the group. None of the recruits had made a single effort to chat with him.

He weighed the options in his mind.

I'm here to serve. What's the worst that could happen? It isn't as if the blokes are speaking to me anyway.

"Mate, the saddle is backward. Look at its shape. The large bit faces back. You are also going to fall off if you don't tighten the girth strap. Pull it taut, and make sure it doesn't move. Just put your fingers under it. That's how you know if it's all right for the horse. Don't worry about making it too tight; the horse will let you know."

"Thanks, mate. I've never been near a horse before in me life. To be honest, I'm still right terrified of them," the grateful recruit said. "Me name's Jack." He offered his hand to Eddie over the low wall.

"I'm Eddie. You have a strong grip. It should serve you well here." He shook his right hand after Jack released it.

Jack looked sheepishly at him. "That's what me da tells me. Blimey, I've been waiting for a proper introduction to you for nearly a week."

Eddie raised his eyebrows in surprise. "Why didn't you say anything? I promise I don't bite."

The jet-black-haired recruit in the stall directly across from them joined in. "Actually, a lot of us have been hesitant. I mean, you're the bloody Prince of Wales." The recruit offered a hand to Eddie. "The name's Vince."

Relief flooded through him. Finally, human interaction! "Fair enough. The name Wales is a bit of a giveaway," Eddie joked.

Glancing to see that Corporal Reed's back was momentarily turned, Vince asked, "Don't you have a code name? I'm sure I speak for all the blokes here, but we all had to sign a bunch of government documents. If they went to that level of detail, you would think they'd want to keep your identity on the down-low."

Eddie grinned. *Just maybe we'll survive this all together.*

"My code name always changes. I can't tell you the current one, but I'm all right with Bond."

"Nah. You ain't a Bond type. We'll come up with something," Jack put forward.

Vince snorted. "For the record, I respect you choosing to enlist over becoming an officer. Shows real grit and determination to be with grunts like us. In my eyes, you're all right, mate. I'm sure you'll convince the naysayers here in time." His eyes lingered on the recruit Corporal Reed was dressing down for being too rough with his horse.

Eddie absorbed the intel. *So that's who my biggest critic is. Interesting.*

The burly recruit was solidly built and broad shouldered like a rugby player. Eddie couldn't remember his name, only that he was from Kent.

Ice broken, he offered a few other short words of advice to those around him. The other recruits were eager for his expertise. He had to hand it to them—the group picked up skills quickly. It wasn't easy beginning with large horses.

Corporal Reed sauntered to each stall, running his hands over each horse, carefully checking the saddle placements, girth tightness, bridle, and overall cleanliness of the horse.

He reached Eddie's stall. "Your horse is still dirty here by the forelegs. Your bridle needs work on the noseband here. See this bit?"

Corporal Reed pointed to a tiny section with his white gloves. Leave it to him to find an area for Eddie to improve upon. "Other than that, well done, Trooper Wales." He nodded and moved on to Jack.

As a member of the Household Cavalry, Eddie would be

expected to perform both ceremonial duties and field duties. When on ceremonial duties, the Household Cavalry Mounted Regiment members lived at Knightsbridge barracks in central London.

They were best known for their daily Changing of the Guards ceremony and Horse Guards Parade. Occasionally, they also performed as the Guard of Honor at official state visits and ceremonies. Being on ceremony duty meant hours upon hours of polishing and cleaning their kits. Eddie shuddered at the thought of what was to come.

Chapter Nineteen

AMANDA

manda: Any word on Princey?

Clara: Sorry, A. Nada. It's the same as the last time you asked. Before you text David, you should know he hasn't spoken to him either. It'll be at least two more weeks before we know anything.

Amanda: It was worth a shot.

Clara: I know you miss him.

Amanda: Written letters aren't enough. Plus, they take forever to get to me.

Clara: I know. I really feel for you, I do. I'd be going nuts if our situations were reversed.

Amanda: I'm trying to stay occupied, but my mind is always thinking about him.

Clara: Because you've fallen for him.

Amanda: I wouldn't say that I've fallen yet… but I'm close. We need to, like, actually date first for that to happen.

Clara: You keep telling yourself that. I'm calling your bluff.

Amanda: *Zipper mouth emoji*

Amanda: I feel like I'm being a bad friend. I haven't actually asked you about you. What's new in the Leeds house?

Clara: Other than busy with Swan Lake rehearsals, not really anything. David's been occupied with his charity projects. Between you and me, he's been a little short tempered. I think Eddie was doing more than he thought and he's only just beginning to realize it.

Amanda: Anything I can do to help?

Clara: I don't think so, at least not yet. He's been cross with his uncle too. Actually… maybe there is something you can do. A visit from you would be the perfect excuse for him to step away from it all.

Amanda: Give me the dates you're both free and I'll make it happen.

Clara: Free? You're funny.

Amanda: Okay, not as busy as normal.

Clara: Doing it now.

Amanda: Screenshotting this. I'll get back to you as soon as I can figure out a couple things.

Clara: Looking forward to it. We miss you.

Over the past two and a half months since she'd last seen Eddie, Amanda had worked flights to Rio, Sydney, Paris, Athens, and Singapore. Her friends and coworkers knew she was always up to work any flights that would take her in the vicinity of the United Kingdom, but so far, nothing had materialized. London was a popular route, and few were ever willing to give it up.

Humming the *Star Wars* tune as she folded her laundry, she thought about Eddie and how he was getting on. Had he remembered how to do his own laundry? Was he used to ironing his uniform and polishing his boots up to the required standard?

I need a photo of him in his uniform for my phone's new lock screen. I bet he looks so handsome.

Suddenly, her phone rang, pulling her out of her thoughts. Dropping her jeans onto the bed, she answered it and held the device to her ear. "This is Amanda."

"Hello, Amanda? This is Melinda, one of the schedulers for Pacific Skyways. Do you have a moment?" The no-nonsense voice made it more of a statement than a question.

Amanda sank down to her bed. "Sure. How can I help you?"

"One of the crew members on tomorrow morning's flight from LAX to Dublin is out on emergency leave. Since you're not scheduled for the next three days, I wanted to reach out to see if you were available to pick up the shift?" She heard the rapid click-clacking of computer keys in the background.

Amanda spent a fraction of a second processing the question. She had to quickly compose herself to sound professional. "Yes, I am fully available."

"Excellent. I'll let the purser know and will forward the itinerary details to your company email account. Thank you." The call disconnected.

Amanda grinned from ear to ear. Finally, a route taking her to Ireland. That was the best news she'd had in a long while. Noting the time, she figured she'd probably better try to catch some shut-eye since she'd have to be up before dawn. Tossing the remaining laundry into the basket, she lay down on the bed without changing and slipped on her eye mask.

I can almost hand deliver Eddie's care package. He wanted Twix bars this time around, but I think I only have Kit Kats. I don't have time to run to the store and pick any up. If he wants American candy, he won't complain.

As her breathing evened out, she fell into a deep sleep,

dreaming of her prince in a red military uniform, riding a magnificent black stallion.

From Irvine, it took her a good hour to make it to the employee parking lot and catch the shuttle to the Pacific Skyways flight-operations area. Passing through the passenger drop-off, Amanda took out her security badge and accessed one of the concealed doors, disguised as a pillar next to the ticketing counter. She hopped into the elevator and headed up to the sixth floor.

The hallways were unremarkable, but behind the third white door on the left-hand side was the "readying room." Incoming crews waited for their briefings before their assigned flights here. Opening the door, Amanda walked into a large room with three wall-to-wall glass windows, providing one of the best views of the LAX runways.

The early morning sun began to rise, illuminating the vintage travel posters adorning the walls on either side of the windows. She placed her bag next to one of the squishy and rather comfortable teal couches.

The roaring sound of the first plane of the day taking off brought her out of her morning haze. Seeing one of the Queen of the Skies, a Boeing 747, taking off into the sunrise made Amanda think about her dad, a retired military turned commercial B-747 pilot.

Wish I could be trained as a cabin crew member on one of those beauties before they retire them.

She sighed. Her last call with her parents hadn't gone well. She could still hear their voices in her head. *"You know, honey, there isn't much of a future for you in aviation. How about you consider going back to school? Your mom and I would be happy to pay for it. We want you to have options. Just in case. You never know what the future might hold."*

She bit her lip. Amanda still considered dropping out of college to attend the flight attendant academy one of the best decisions she'd ever made. She'd been able to see so much of the world. She personally had no regrets.

Maybe if did go back and earn my college degree, it would get them off my back. The ironic thing is that flying literally runs in my blood. You'd think Mom and Dad would understand that and be at peace with my decision. I'm happy. I love my job.

One by one, the other fifteen crew members trickled into the lounge. The volume of voices steadily rose as they also enjoyed their own morning beverages. Amanda munched on a granola bar and fruit as she glanced over the cheat sheet of VIPs and notes for the day. She was ecstatic to read they would be servicing a brand-new plane to the Pacific Skyways fleet, an Airbus A-350.

One way to pass the time inside the lounge was to exchange gossip from the past few days. Most of the stories could never leave the lounge. If the airline executives ever found out what really happened on the clock, it would be a swift departure from the company.

When it got particularly slow on the plane, the cabin crew sometimes played passenger bingo. Crew members tried to find intoxicated passengers, confused passengers, sleepy passengers, and the like to complete their bingo cards.

Amanda listened in. "Have you heard that Captain Dan forgot his glasses in Phoenix, and they had to delay the Houston outbound flight until another pilot from the next Phoenix flight could get them delivered back to him? Unbelievable. What would our passengers say if they ever heard? I felt so bad telling them we had a weather delay," joked one of Amanda's friends.

"Are you serious? The captain forgot his glasses? I have one for you," said the only male flight attendant, Drew. "This wasn't this week, though. It was two weeks ago. Captain Jack misread his flight plan and took flight 737 to SNA instead of SAN. It's not that easy to mix up the Orange County and San Diego airport codes."

Amanda had heard about this one. "It's a good thing it was only a ferry flight and there weren't any passengers on the plane," she said. "What's really sad is that Captain Jack had a brand-new first officer who didn't want to overstep their bounds and was afraid to say anything."

She shook her head and laughed with mirth, having to wipe tears from her eyes. In a ferry flight, the plane was empty and was only being moved from one location to another.

Dad's flown to the wrong place before. Not the first person for that to happen to.

"Well, it sounds like everyone is ready for a good flight today," a cheerful voice announced as the room grew silent.

Amanda felt her body stiffen. Irene was their purser for the flight from LAX to DUB. The tall, svelte blonde was one of the most relaxed and experienced pursers around, but she didn't get along well with Amanda. They could work professionally together, but would never be friends. Amanda had earned the top spot in their flight attendant training class many years ago. Irene had held a grudge ever since.

"Sorry for the delay. I hit an accident on the 710 from Long Beach. Anyhow, let's do a quick roll call. I have some notes to review before we head out to the gate." Irene placed her belongings down and stood in front of the assembled crew members.

All the flight attendants checked in for roll call. Amanda's mind was only half paying attention to the news and notes she was supposed to be aware of. She had asked to be on this flight. She could handle a couple of hours with Irene, couldn't she? Would Irene banish her to work in the economy cabin?

Chapter Twenty

AMANDA

As Amanda ran through the economy galley checklist, she wondered how more than half of the crew had gotten placed on the Dublin route. They were all newbies. She had more seniority than all of them put together!

It took me two years to earn my way up to international routes. These guys haven't even been with the airline for six months.

Yvette, a newer flight attendant, approached her. "Collins, looks like you're stuck with me in economy. Sorry. Are you going to consider a transfer to Europe? It sounds just up your alley. I might even give it a go myself, except my husband would kill me."

Amanda froze. "European transfer? What are you talking about?" How had she not heard the news? She'd been putting out feelers for any UK-based routes.

"What Irene was going around and asking people about earlier. There's a short window of opportunity to transfer to one of the extended European bases of operations. I think she said London and Paris were the focus hubs. Are you going to have her recommend you?"

Yvette kept speaking, but Amanda again tuned out everything around her. Why hadn't Irene mentioned this to her and what did Yvette mean by recommendation? She clenched her jaw.

"I'm confused. I swear I didn't see anything like this posted on the employee site. I've been hounding it for weeks." Amanda placed her clipboard down and leaned against the galley counter.

"The application is only open to the pursers. They're the ones who fill out who's interested in transferring. Who do you normally work with? Actually, you probably don't have time; the deadline to let them put your name forward is tonight. They only asked crews that work certain routes. You should ask Irene." Yvette chuckled at her curious expression.

Amanda face-palmed and cringed. She'd have to ask Irene for a favor. This was important. Would Irene do it for her? If not, who could she ask?

"I also heard a rumor about downsizing some of the more senior flight attendants from my hubby," Yvette added. "Have you heard anything?"

Amanda's eyes bulged. Now what was she speaking about?

"Nope. Let's do the economy blanket and pillow check. You can catch me up on the other news as we work. Sounds like I've been out of the loop."

Amanda had to ensure all of the seat-back tables were upright, free of garbage, and that each seat had a clean blanket, headset, and pillow. They split the aisles up and worked across from one another.

Yvette loved to chatter, but she provided an excellent wealth of information. "Pacific Skyways is in big trouble financially. My husband works as a consultant to one of the chief financial officers. They way overspent on their expansion plans. This is a secret, but the airline is looking to cut costs wherever they can. They've already started looking at the pilots close to retirement. We're next. There's a hiring freeze on cabin crew."

Amanda's mind wandered. So the airline wasn't doing well? What did that mean for her? She had five years with the company under her belt. Should she look into working for another airline? What about her father? Did he have any relevant information? Perhaps she needed to call home.

The second it was safe to do so, Amanda turned on her cell and sent a few quick messages off to Clara. The clock on her phone switched over to Greenwich Mean Time, eight hours ahead of California's Pacific Standard Time.

Amanda: It's been the world's longest flight. Fill you in when I can. We still on for some girl time?

Clara: I've been waiting for you to message me. Have you landed yet? Of course I'm ready. I want to hear everything!

Amanda: Landing in Dublin now. About to clean the cabin, then catch the hopper to Gatwick. See you in a couple hours.

After almost fourteen hours on the job—eleven in flight and the remainder on the ground—Amanda was eager to be off duty. She'd have two days of free time before her next flight back to the States from Paris. She intended to use every moment to de-stress. Alongside being given the most unenviable tasks by the cabin crew supervisor, she also had to deal with a fair number of grumpy passengers.

Amanda quickly conducted her last cabin inspection, checking for any valuable or children's items that were left behind. The rest of the crew did the same as the cleaners boarded to prepare the plane to return home to LAX in two hours' time. She searched for an opening to have a quick word with Irene.

Her stomach knotted with anxiety. Time was running out. As they reached the jet bridge, Irene thanked the fifteen members of the crew and debriefed them while they waited for the pilots and first officers to finish their paperwork. It was now or never.

"Do you think I can have a quick word with you?" Amanda said hesitantly, approaching the blonde supervisor.

Irene nodded and motioned for her to step out of earshot of the other flight attendants near the business-class galley. Amanda fidgeted, shifting her weight from one foot to another.

"I've heard that there's the possibility of a transfer to our London or Paris ops base."

Irene narrowed her eyes. "Yes, that's accurate. What do you want to know, Collins?" Her tone was flat, but professional.

Her breathing quickened. "Look, I understand we aren't on the best of terms, but I'd appreciate it if you could recommend me for a transfer. I'm always professional, a hard worker, and I never shy away from my responsibilities. I'm cross-trained on the B-767, B-777, B-787, A 330, and A-350."

Irene studied her for a moment. "I'll agree with you on those counts, but let me ask you this: You already work two of the prime LA-based routes to Paris and Zurich. Don't you think it would be better to give someone else the opportunity for career advancement?"

"No. I have to look out for my own interests too," she replied, wincing at the selfish-sounding words. However, it was the answer that Irene seemed to want.

Irene raised her eyebrow. "That's the first time I've ever heard you give that type of an answer. To be honest, I've heard through the grapevine you wanted a change. I've always been jealous of how easily everything has come to you in the flight-attendant world. You are so relaxed with all types of people and can have anyone listen to you. I never had the gift of being calm all the time like you. That being said, I want you to understand that Pac Skyways has shifted its eligibility requirements for transfers. I can recommend you, but be aware that you may not pass muster."

Amanda frowned. "What's changed?"

The pilots were wrapping up their paperwork and about to join the group by the plane's main door. They only had a few more moments. "Pac Skyways recently added a requirement that all internationally based FAs have a college degree or the equivalent foreign language competency."

Amanda understood exactly where Irene was coming from. Her heart dropped. "Thank you for giving me a straight answer."

They held one another's gaze for a moment before Irene indicated they should rejoin the group. The pilot and copilot smiled and nodded to the crew as they came out from the cockpit with their coats and rolling packs.

"We're ready to go, then?" Irene said. The group exited the plane, Amanda feeling even more uncertain as to what her future might hold.

Amanda was officially back at London Gatwick. The weather was blustery, and it felt as if it might snow. She followed the crowds to the taxi stand and shivered as she sent off a quick text.

Amanda: Why didn't you tell me it was so cold here? I would've packed winter clothing. Getting a cab now. Meet you at the Borough Market as planned.

Clara: Finishing rehearsal. You're a seasoned traveler! You didn't think to check the weather app?

Amanda: Must have slipped my mind.

Clara: If you need extra layers, you can borrow from me.

Amanda: *Smiling emoji* See you in a bit.

Pulling her jacket closer to her body, Amanda all but scampered over to the black cabbie the moment it approached.

"Welcome to London, miss. Where are ye heading off to today?" the driver asked as he assisted her with her well-traveled rolling luggage.

"Thanks! Borough Market, please." The driver nodded as Amanda rubbed her hands together for warmth.

Chapter Twenty-One

EDDIE

I n the Windsor riding school over the past few weeks, the recruits had all learned to walk, trot, and canter in formation. Before they moved down to London, where they would be close to graduating, or "passing out" as it was better known, the trainees all needed to learn how to jump. Today's efforts were spectacularly horrible.

Eddie shuddered as the recruits moved their horses through the jumping lane again. Every single one of them had now fallen off at least twice. He grumbled. His ego was bruised more than his body. If there was a weak point to Eddie's horsemanship, it was jumping. He didn't have the natural ability like his sister. As always, the horses appeared to have a mind of their own.

Eddie patted his horse and used him to take his place at the top of the jumping lane. He took a few deep breaths and prepared himself.

Leaning forward, he murmured to Freddy, "You're trying to make me look bad, aren't you? If you don't let me stay in my seat this time, no extra ration of carrots."

Eddie pulled the reins and squeezed his thighs against the

horse, urging him into a canter. Freddy picked up speed. He approached the first and second jumps just fine. On the third jump, Freddy suddenly decided he didn't want to go over the rail and stopped. Eddie went flying off the saddle, rolling on the ground. Freddy came up to his fist and licked it.

"No treats."

Resounding laughter filled Eddie's ears. His face grew red with heat as he groaned.

"Trooper Wales! Again!" Corporal Reed commanded.

"Yes, sir."

"Wales, it's nice to see you suffer like the rest of us," Vince rubbed in later that night. The recruits liked calling Eddie "Wales," and he didn't mind it one bit.

"My bum does not take to staying in my saddle. It's electric." Eddie winced as he sat on his bed. His backside needed a respite from the hard ground.

Ah bugger, I need to do laundry again. He glanced at his pile of uniforms.

"Anyone doing their washing tonight? It appears I can't avoid it." All his clothes were covered in dirt. The last thing Eddie wanted was to be called out by the corporal for a dirty uniform.

"I did mine last week, mate," Vince replied. "So did Jack. You're on your own."

Eddie shrugged. "All right, mate, don't say I didn't offer."

Vince laughed.

Slowly straightening himself up, Eddie dug through his trunk and pulled out a few other items that needed to be washed.

A knock on the door caused everyone in the barracks to jump to immediate attention. Only the officers knocked.

"At ease, men. Trooper Wales, you have a visitor in my office." Visitor was the code word for protection officer. The corporal looked to Eddie and nodded, indicating he should follow.

Questions and scenarios ran through his mind. *What's happened? Why is Jon here? Is it my parents? Is it David? Has there been an attack?*

Eddie forced himself to take a deep breath. There was no need to jump to conclusions yet. The commanding officer led him from the barracks to the officer's administrative area.

"Trooper Wales, inform me when you've completed your meeting. I shall be in the room next door."

"Thank you, sir. I will." He saluted his commander, who turned and exited.

Jonathan stood as Eddie entered the room. He cleared his throat. His clothing was slightly askew. Something was definitely up. Jonathan never dressed less than perfect. Eddie remained standing and frowned.

"Sir, I'm sorry to pull you away from your duties."

He gulped. The muscles in his stomach clenched. "Jon, what's happened?"

"There's been an accident," Jonathan began.

He'd learned a lot about coping techniques and mechanisms after his breakup with his last girlfriend. His heart began to race. Jonathan never held anything back from him.

"An accident? What do you mean? I need details." Eddie forced himself to focus, his mind threatening to spiral into panic. "Give me a moment." He placed his hand on his chest, attempting to steady his racing heart. Jonathan sympathetically offered him a glass of water before he delivered the news.

"Ms. Collins was involved in a car accident after leaving London's Gatwick airport earlier today. Let me stress that she is all right. The hospital contacted Ms. Little, who immediately rang Leeds and me. Ms. Collins's parents have been contacted, as well as His Majesty, due to the nature of your relationship with her." Jonathan paused.

"Amanda!" He resisted the urge to run over to the door, yank it open, and race down to London.

A thin layer of perspiration formed on his brow. "Is she in serious condition? Stable? Was she driving? Tell me every detail you are aware of." Eddie leaned forward on the edge of his seat.

"The taxi carrying Ms. Collins was struck by another taxi. She is stable, but they are still assessing her injuries. My last update came from Leeds an hour ago. It could have been much more serious. The king requested Dr. Evans check in as a consultant on the case. Leeds will update us when we have more information." Jonathan motioned for Eddie to have another drink from the glass of water. "I was also informed by His Majesty himself that you won't receive any leave until you are eligible for it in three days' time."

Eddie jumped to his feet in protest and paced the room.

How does Father think I can get through this? He expects me to be able to focus? Wait until I tell him exactly what I think about all this.

Eddie needed to be a solid figure. He was being selfish. What about Amanda's family? She mentioned her parents in Seattle. Were they on their way? What about once they reached London? He wasn't the only one experiencing panic, fear, guilt, and desperation all at once.

Her parents had to be at their wit's end with panic. Eddie needed to take control of the situation. If there was anything he'd learned from Amanda, it was that you couldn't worry about things beyond the realm of your control.

As if sensing his thoughts, Jonathan changed his tone, his voice softening. "Eddie, I promise she is receiving the best possible care. That's why we were slow to advise you of the situation. You know I'll inform you the moment I get wind of any changes."

"It's scary sometimes how you can just read my mind." He exhaled deeply. "Please inform her that the moment I'm released from my duties, I'll be on my way her."

I wish I could go now, but Amanda would get upset at me for not finishing my training. She knows how important this is.

"Can you ensure I have a clean suit in my bag when the car comes to take me to the hospital on Wednesday? Oh, and my mobile." Eddie continued to pace the room to expel his nervous and emotional energy.

"Of course. Anything else I can do for you, sir?" Jonathan asked.

"No. That's it."

It wouldn't do well to show his father any childish behavior. He'd handle this like a mature man and see his duties through. That was the way to prove to his parents that he'd changed, especially if he wanted them to accept Amanda when they finally met her.

Amanda, hold on. I'll be there as soon as I can. I promise nothing will stand in my way.

Chapter Twenty-Two

AMANDA

Monitors beeped in the background, and the scent of antiseptic hung heavy in the air. Shapes around her moved about, but everything was fuzzy and out of focus. Sounds seemed distorted. Amanda's eyelids felt heavy. She closed them, drifting back asleep.

The next time she opened her eyes, her vision was still blurred, but this time she was more aware of her surroundings.

Well, I'm obviously in a hospital. It smells too clean to be anywhere else. I wouldn't be surprised if my bruises have bruises. Is my vision always going to be blurry like this?

Her head hurt. Taking inventory of her aches and pains, Amanda dearly hoped she hadn't scared anyone too badly.

I need to get ahold of work. They're not going to like this. I didn't pack much... better pick up some new clothes when I'm released. I'm still in London, I think.

"Ah, our patient is awake!" A low, cheery Irish voice broke Amanda's train of thoughts. He was examining her chart. "Miss Collins. It's nice to see you finally in the land of the conscious. You have had quite a few people here to see you—

on pins and needles with worry—the last couple of hours. You are in London at St. Mary's Hospital."

Amanda couldn't quite make out the face, but he appeared to be in his mid-forties and had slightly balding red hair.

"Sorry if I don't get up. I don't think I can even if I wanted to. You seem to know me, but who are you? What's happened?" Amanda wracked her brain. Had she met this doctor before? Or was it a nurse?

The stranger chuckled. "I'm Dr. Evans. You've been in a car accident."

She knew that name! He was the kindly doctor who treated Clara when she was injured about eight months before. Clara had nothing but positive experiences and glowing reviews of the good doctor. She vaguely remembered something about his daughter.

She was surprised he would treat her, however. Somebody royal must have called in his services. She frowned, unable to remember exactly why she was in London.

"Is everyone okay?" she asked.

"Indeed. It could have been much worse. Your driver injured his leg. I believe he was just released from the fracture clinic. How are you feeling, Miss Collins? And your pain level, if I may ask?"

Dr. Evans went through a quick examination of her senses, head, and body. Amanda felt as if she didn't have full control over her own limbs.

She was relieved to hear the driver wasn't seriously injured. She was still fuzzy on the details. Amanda closed her eyes and focused. All she succeeded in doing was making herself more irritated at her inability to recall the full events earlier in the day. She assumed she had been working a flight.

"Please try and refrain from moving your right arm.

There's a heavy cast on it," Dr. Evans advised. She squinted at the large plaster cast on her arm.

"I feel as if I have had some bricks laid on me and then a concrete foundation on top of that. I'd say I'm at about an eight out of ten. I hurt, but that means I'm alive and kicking. No complaints. Just let me know when I can get out of here."

She felt downcast. Her ability to banter usually helped to lift her spirits. She was having to reach deep to try to stay somewhat positive. "Actually," she said. "There is one concern. Is it normal for my vision to be blurry? I should have twenty-twenty vision." Amanda imagined the blurry doctor to be smiling at her sassy rebuttals.

"Do you have a headache?"

She closed her eyes against the brightness of the penlight. Paper shuffled, and a pen made some marks against her medical chart. Amanda shook her head to say no and quickly regretted the action. All the muscles in her neck tensed and spasmed. "Ow. I shouldn't have done that."

Dr. Evans carefully placed a hand on her neck and gently massaged the area. "Probably not. The muscles in your neck and back are especially tender. No sudden movements. In your case, yes, it is common to have blurry vision. Among your injuries is a grade-two concussion from the impact."

"That stinks. I am not the most patient patient," Amanda mumbled.

"Indeed. Your family and friends have been giving the staff of St. Mary's a fair bit of stress. I daresay they're not very patient either." Dr. Evans moved over to Amanda's right side, took her pulse, checked his watch, and scribbled down another note.

"Now that you mention it, what's the total damage here? Anything going to keep me in the hospital longer than necessary? Do I need surgery?" Amanda was ready for her own soft bed and some nice, soft silk sheets. Traveling a lot made a girl spoiled.

"Your injuries have been primarily to your shoulder. We call the long bone in the shoulder the humerus. You've fractured the head, or top of it, where it inserts into the joint socket. Once the swelling goes down, we can have a couple scans done to assess the ligaments, tendons, and soft tissue."

Dr. Evans paused. "If recovery is smooth, I anticipate six to twelve weeks before the bone is healed. Normal range of motion can be regained in approximately three to six months. You should be released from the hospital tomorrow."

How was she going to get through the long healing period? She was right-handed. There was no way she was going to be able to work anytime soon. How was she going to support herself?

Amanda felt anxious. The pressure on the front part of her head began to increase.

Dr. Evans noted her discomfort. "I'm going to offer you some more pain medication. At present, I am not ready to clear you to travel back to America until I am satisfied with your beginning stages of recovery. As I mentioned, concussions can be unpredictable. In the meantime, please try not to jostle your arm. I can't place a cast over the shoulder, only the humerus. You will have to become accustomed to sleeping upright or solely on your back."

It took her a few moments, but Amanda felt Dr. Evans's words sinking in. She wasn't allowed to travel? Her emotions rapidly changed from nervous to happy.

"That's humorous! You mean you are requiring me to stay in lovely London for the immediate time being?" She would jump up and down, giddy, if she could.

"When you look at it from that perspective, I suppose I am. Do you have any additional questions?"

She had none. Amanda was surprised to find it had only been a day and a half since her accident. There were periods where she had been awake, but all the details were incoherent. Time moved at a different speed when you were unaware of what was going on.

It was late afternoon when Dr. Evans departed; visiting hours were almost over for the day. She was an exception to the rules, however, and immediately perked up as David and Clara passed the departing doctor. Amanda used the controls on her bed to move it into a more upright position.

She was tired, but Clara and David were ohana. Ohana meant family. She put a cheesy grin on her face and greeted them. "Welcome to my humble abode." It wasn't difficult to discern, even with her fuzzy vision, the tall blond prince and her petite best friend.

"Amanda! You had me worried to death! Don't you ever get into an accident again! I'll bubble wrap you myself if I have to and roll you everywhere I go in an armored car padded with high-density foam," Clara exclaimed as she parked herself in the chair next to Amanda. David shook his head and remained standing behind his fiancée.

A small hint of panic jumped through her brain. Clara lost her adoptive parents to a car accident. *Is she okay? Am I the trigger of extra stress or the horrid memories?*

"Clara. Are you all right?"

"I'm fine. I panicked at first, like I said, but I have David," she offered. Amanda let out a breath she didn't know she was holding.

"You had us both worried," David added in his baritone voice. "I'm happy to see you're still the same quirky person I text every now and again. I promised Eddie I'd let you know that he will be here the moment he receives his three-day pass."

Amanda quivered at hearing Eddie's name. He was so close! It was coming back to her. He was in Windsor training.

She knew it was unreasonable for him to leave his army training just like that, but she wanted nothing more than to just have him sit next to her and be there. Even thinking about Eddie relaxed her. She could rest her aching head on his broad chest and have him play with her hair.

"How are you feeling?" David continued.

"Rotten, but happy you're both here to see my humorous situation."

"Oh… I am sorry to hear that?" His voice rose in uncertainty. She could imagine him wondering why her situation was supposed to be funny.

"My humerus is broken." Amanda grinned.

Clara face-palmed.

David muttered something that sounded like "very punny."

"Anyway… look at what I brought," Clara said, displaying a petite wicker basket with the letters 'F' and 'M' etched on it.

"Oh, Fortnum and Mason! Does that hamper have any mince pies in it?"

"Of course." Clara gently ran her hand through Amanda's hair. "This is a hot mess. I may need a stronger-bristle brush than the one I brought to untangle this bird's nest."

She ignored the comment. "What else is in there?"

"What do you think?" Clara set it down and extracted several jars and packages. "Jam, tea, scones, honey, biscuits, chocolates, and a couple other pastries."

Amanda was touched by all the trouble Clara had gone to take care of her. She was one of those people she could always count on, through thick or thin. She'd missed having her bestie by her side. She found it difficult to process all her emotions.

"So that's why the hamper was so heavy," David chimed in, giving the girls puppy-dog eyes. "Any chance you two ladies could spare a couple biscuits for your favorite shoemaker?"

"That's up to A," Clara said, rolling her eyes.

"I can share everything except the chocolate," Amanda offered with a smile. "The bars are small, and I'd like them to last as long as possible."

The three savored the prepacked mince pies and hot tea from Clara's travel coffee mug. David apologized for having to cut his visit short—he was due to meet with the king and update him on Amanda's health. Kissing Clara goodbye, he departed, leaving the two best friends to their own devices.

"Okay, C, if you're up for brushing my hair, please use detangler first."

Amanda was thankful Clara could help her feel more human again.

"I'll be gentle, A, and especially mindful of your neck. Dr. Evans said the muscles are going to be extra tender for a while. I'll brush as many curls as I can reach."

"I appreciate you. There's one other thing I wanted to ask…" She hesitated. "Do you have a mirror? I know I probably have a ton of bruises, but I need to see the damage with my own eyes."

Wordlessly, Clara handed a compact mirror to Amanda.

"Yowzah." She winced. Two purplish eyes and some greenish-purple bruises started back to her. She quickly snapped the mirror shut, feeling her breathing intensify. "I look like I went ten rounds with a boxer," she lamented, her self-confidence plummeting.

"It'll heal in time. Be patient. You're still a stunning redhead. You can think about that *I Love Lucy* episode where Lucy has a black eye."

Amanda appreciated Clara's efforts to make her feel better. She sighed. "Thank you, C." She changed the subject. "Any word on Eddie? And you weren't kidding about David. He looks really stressed out."

"I heard from David that poor Eddie has been chomping

at the bit to get down to the hospital and see you. He'll be here tomorrow. We're hoping that's when you'll be released, and we can take you home. I'm sure you have a lot to catch up on," Clara said.

Amanda sighed. *I wish he were here now. His soothing voice reading is just what I need. I wonder if he'd be game to watch some classic TV shows like my beloved Lucy?*

"I'd be furious if he jeopardized his training over me, so I'm glad he's staying the course." Amanda repositioned some of her hair. "And if you're going to work on the curls, you may also need some leave-in conditioner. With a cast, showering is going be a pain."

"Don't worry. I'm a seasoned pro at wrapping a cast." Clara rummaged through her toiletry kit. "Oh, and a word of warning…" Her friend shook her head. "The apartment is a mess. I'm starting to think David's a pack rat, given the number of files and papers that seem to find a home on every flat surface. He won't delegate any Waleeds stuff. I'm not sure what to do other than mandate a 'no work after six' rule."

Amanda could hear the strain in her voice. She closed her eyes, letting the comforting sensation of Clara brushing her hair soothe her. "I know my parents are probably around too. Have they driven you up a wall yet? Oh, and I need to reach out to work and let them know I'm going to be out for a while."

"Your parents are staying in Central London. You know I adore them; they could never drive me crazy," Clara assured her.

"Has mom gone out shopping yet?"

"Has she?" Clara laughed. "Yesterday, when we knew you'd be out of it for a while, she went out at ten and wasn't back until eight. And today, she went out again for another hour to hit more shops. I don't know how she finds the energy."

"Shopping is Mom's stress relief."

Eddie is going to love my mom. I just hope I have a chance to run interference between him and Dad before they meet.

If Amanda had one fear, it was that her dad would scare Eddie away from her.

Chapter Twenty-Three

EDDIE

The three days waiting to be released to travel down to London were the longest of Eddie's life. He didn't recall eating or sleeping much as he mechanically went through his training. He isolated himself from the world, consumed by his thoughts. Despite his withdrawal, his fellow recruits did their best to cover for him, empathizing with his situation.

"Wales. You do understand you are part of the brotherhood, right, mate? If you need us, all you have to do is let us know. We can lend you a couple of ears, mate," Leon, one of the quieter recruits, offered.

"Yeah, and we promise whatever you tell us stays in this room. If there is one lesson we're learning here, it's that we have to trust one another. We'll all be serving together for at least the next four years, mate. We're one another's second family," Vince added.

Leon and Vince are right. I know bottling my emotions isn't healthy.

"I'm sorry for being such a miserable companion. This is

the first time I've had someone close to me get hurt. I've never felt so helpless. I'm here and my girl's in the hospital."

He opened up to them on his inner thoughts and turmoil. Having others understand his situation made him feel more human and as if he wasn't alone. They really were becoming a family.

Early the next morning, Eddie stood in the hospital hallway just outside of Amanda's room, waiting for his security team to finish its routine sweep. He readjusted his tie and brushed his hand down the soft fabric of his navy-blue suit.

"All clear, sir," Jon said.

"Thank you."

Eddie took a deep breath and reached for the door handle leading to Amanda's room. Just as he did so, a man with thinning red hair and immaculately polished shoes emerged. His sharp green eyes bore directly into Eddie's. Blocking the doorway, he crossed his arms and looked Eddie over, probably searching for any sign of weakness. There was no mistaking who this man was.

Refusing to be intimidated, Eddie stood tall and extended his hand. "Hello, Mr. Collins. My name is Edmund, or Eddie. It's a pleasure to meet you, though I wish it were under better circumstances."

Mr. Collins briefly shook his hand. "I can't say the same is true from my point of view, Edmund," he said sharply. "Imagine my surprise to receive a call that my daughter has been in an accident and has a new boyfriend all at the same time."

After facing my drill sergeant, I can handle this.

Eddie tried not to wince, empathizing with the shock that

must have come to Amanda's parents. He remembered the dread and terror of the last few days. Mr. Collins was well within his rights to be upset given the circumstances.

"No, sir. I expect not."

"I'll let you in to see Amanda since she's been asking for you…" Mr. Collins took a half step forward. Eddie didn't move a muscle. "But let's be clear. I will not tolerate *any* funny business with my daughter or her best friend. I consider Clara to be my second daughter."

"Understood," Eddie replied, swallowing hard. "Both women are exceedingly special. With Amanda, our relationship may still be new, but I've never met a person like her. Neither of us knows where our relationship will take us, but rest assured, she will *always* be treated with respect and like the treasure she is."

Not to mention she'll also always be protected by my security team, but it's probably best not to bring that up right now. I don't need him to worry about the endless lists of security threats that come with dating me.

Eddie made an effort to maintain eye contact with Mr. Collins, consciously controlling his blinking.

I am the man he can count on to take care of her.

"Tom, are finished trying to scare off Amanda's boyfriend? She's been waiting for him to come in."

Mr. Collins turned and stepped away from the doorway as a woman a tad shorter than Amanda exited the hospital room, closing the door behind her. She sported the same curly red hair as her daughter. Mrs. Collins wore a black top and silk floral scarf around her neck. Her accent caught him off guard. She was English.

Mr. Collins gave his wife a sheepish look and cleared his throat. "Darling, we were just having a little chat to get to know one another better. Weren't we, Edmund?"

"Oh, you were, were you?" Amanda's mother placed her hands on her hips.

"No, ma'am. We were discussing my conduct and how I should treat your daughter," Eddie clarified. "As I was about to tell your husband, ma'am, I'm one of the newest recruits in His Majesty's Household Cavalry. I was only granted leave for a few days. If we're finished with this inquisition, I'd appreciate being able to spend some of my valuable time with your daughter."

He noticed a glimmer of respect in Mr. Collins's eyes.

"I appreciate your honesty, Your Royal Highness. We won't keep you," Mrs. Collins said.

"I would greatly appreciate it if you called me Edmund or Eddie." He extended his hand to her. "If you do not mind me asking… your accent. Where in England are you originally from?"

"My parents resided in Manchester for many years," Mrs. Collins replied, offering Eddie a warm smile as she shook his hand and then touched her husband's arm. "I can't believe my little girl is dating *you*! Amanda has harbored a crush on you since she was a little girl. She's always kept magazine cutouts and articles about you in her little scrapbook." She paused and smiled fondly at the memory.

I'm never going to let Amanda hear the end of this.

"Have Amanda pass me your address when you're settled into your first posting. Having been a military wife, I know exactly the type of care packages you boys need."

Interesting. Amanda must've taken after her mom personality-wise. Was this where she learned her tricks of the trade?

Having recovered from his earlier faux pas, Mr. Collins rejoined the conversation. "You've managed to pass my test, young man. You will still need to earn my trust. However, you're well on your way." Eddie wholeheartedly agreed with Amanda's father, who pecked his wife with a kiss on the cheek.

Turning back to Eddie, he asked, "Which division are you serving in? I had several acquaintances within the RAF and Army when I was stationed here with the Air Force."

"The Life Guards, sir. It's the oldest division in the British Army. I have a few weeks of riding school remaining before my regiment settles into ceremonial duties here in London."

An idea suddenly inspired Eddie. "Would you two like to meet my parents while you're here in the UK?"

Meeting the king had to earn him some brownie points, at least with Mrs. Collins. She was still British by birth. The sense of ceremony should appeal to her. Amanda's mother didn't show any fuss, but smiled and thanked Eddie for the gesture. "We would love to, but only if they can accommodate us. I'm sure they are exceptionally busy people."

"I'll have one of my parents' private secretaries ring you later today. If you'd like a tour of the palace, I'd also be happy to offer either myself or my cousin to serve as your personal tour guide."

I helped David out with Clara last time, so it's his turn to help me.

"Thank you." Mrs. Collin beamed.

He rocked back and forth on his heels, bouncing in eager anticipation.

I don't want to be rude. How much small talk is enough?

Picking up on Eddie's body language, Mrs. Collins said, "Of course you want to see my little girl. Please, go inside. Tom and I are in need of a proper tea service while you visit. Tell her we'll return later this afternoon when she's released. It has been a while since I've been down to Harrods. We'll take tea there and maybe even do a little shopping."

"More shopping? Just how do you expect to get all the purchases you've already picked up home?" Mr. Collins groaned. "At this rate, we might as well rent a plane and have me fly it home."

"That might not be such a bad idea," Mrs. Collins mused. She directed her husband down the hall. Like a good soldier, he followed.

Eddie shook his head and, at long last, made his way into Amanda's room.

Chapter Twenty-Four

AMANDA

Amanda was groggy and tired of her parents. She appreciated their intentions in dropping everything to fly over to London to see her, but she needed space. Their reunion meeting had been emotionally draining for both parties. They were finally past the awkward stage and on relatively good terms again.

Over the past day, her vision had improved, though it still fell short of where she wanted it to be. Nonetheless, it was a big improvement from the squinting. She continued to battle a persistent headache.

Following the concussion protocol, Amanda was barred from watching television or using her phone. Even reading was limited. Between her visitors, with nothing to do, she had ample time to contemplate the future.

Question one: How was she going to support herself?

If I can't lift fifty pounds of luggage, I can't work. I have maybe one or two months of money in my savings account.

Her mood darkened at the possibility of the long-term implications of her accident and the possibility of having no choice in changing careers.

Question two: If she couldn't fly, what could she do? Flying was so much of who she was. Her parents had been right.

I guess I could look for something in hospitality if I had to. Maybe I could work at a hotel or something. I have a ton of experience working with people.

A knock on the door signaled a visitor's arrival. Amanda suddenly became more alert. Could it be Eddie? Her heart began to race. The door opened. Although still blurry, her eyes settled on the tall sandy-haired man rushing into the room. This wasn't how she'd pictured their reunion, but none of it mattered. Eddie was here!

"Eddie!" Amanda's voice had risen three octaves. "I've been waiting for you for so long!"

She wanted to see his face and convey to him just how much she had missed him. She sat up as best she could. In two strides, Eddie crossed the room and breathlessly stood next to her bed.

Taking her good hand, he began planting kisses all the way up it. When he reached her face, he cupped her cheeks with his hands and tenderly kissed her on the lips. Amanda closed her eyes and sighed in pure bliss.

"I've missed you so much, Princey. You're the world's best medicine."

"I've missed you too, Collins." Eddie remained quiet, and Amanda assumed he was assessing the extent of her injuries. He gently brushed his fingers over the darker, mottled patches of bruised skin around her body, which had become more pronounced over the last day.

The last thing I need is to add more stress to Eddie. There is nothing he can do about these bruises.

"About time you come to the rescue. Mom is at the point of talking about all the yarn she picked up at Liberty of London. I need more stimulating conversation. I've counted the number of tiles on the ceiling like three times now. I don't have Clara to text or check my phone for me. I know it's cruel to speak about them that way, and I do love them, but there is a reason I'm in LA and they are in Seattle."

She took a deep breath. "I hope my parents didn't put you off me. Mom is already in love with you, by the way. She thinks we're the best royal love story of all time. I hope she didn't mention my yearly calendar of you, did she? Or the playing cards? Oh snap… I have no filter on what is coming out of my mouth right now. I'd better just stop talking while you don't think I'm super crazy."

For the first time in months, she was finally able to see Eddie in real life. He *had* changed. He had always been proud, but now he exuded a different type of confidence. He carried himself differently, more upright, with his shoulders back.

Perhaps the most noticeable change, though, was behind Eddie's eyes. A newfound look of maturity gleamed within. Amanda could see that they shimmered with emotions—angst, concern, worry, and relief.

"Amanda. Hearing you speak is the most beautiful sound to me in the world. I hear your voice in my dreams. The last few weeks have been torture to me, but the last three days especially. I've been ready to steal one of the horses, abandon my training course, and have it gallop down to the hospital to see you."

Emotion poured out of Eddie's words. A small tear rolled down his cheek. Amanda felt it hit her hand as he rested his head on her hand.

"Oh, mi amour. I'm not worth crying over. I'm here and still in a few pieces. I'm not going anywhere anytime soon. I'm kind of hoping David and Clara wouldn't mind hosting me at their place to recover, but I'm a Collins. We're built to last." Amanda gently brushed the flyaway hairs off the top of Eddie's head and planted a sweet kiss.

I want nothing more than to cuddle with my precious prince. As soon as I can, that is the number one thing on my to-do list.

"Don't ever say that. Now I have to ask, before we go along any further, how are you doing? I understand if you'd rather I didn't ask, but for my own mental health, I need to know."

Eddie looked up and adjusted Amanda's blanket to tuck her in. She wiggled out of the blanket and patted the bed with her good arm. He took the hint. Taking off his shoes, he carefully slid his large six-foot-plus frame into the bed as it dipped down under his weight. He just fit. Everything felt so right when Eddie was next to her.

"Much better." Amanda sighed. "This is the closest I can get to cuddling with you. I knew you'd want to know. Always to the point. The upper bone in my arm, where it connects to the shoulder, and a couple of ribs are busted. My vision is fuzzy, but I'll heal. Comes with having a concussion. I'm really lucky not to be worse off. On the bright side, I'm stuck here in London with you."

Eddie listened intently. "Thank you for giving me a full answer, A. I feel much better." He sounded relieved to hear Amanda's diagnosis from her. His eyes shifted to a lighter blue color.

Methodically, Eddie rubbed circles on Amanda's left hand. "When you're released, I'm going to make you a nice dinner. We can do whatever you want tonight as long as you let me take care of you. It's my turn to be your host."

Amanda rested her head on his chest, careful not to jar her still-tender neck muscles. His stubble felt rough against her skin. "You look like you need to shower, shave, and take a catnap. Now that you've seen I'm fine, your girlfriend is officially giving you the boot to do all three of those things."

"I only have two and a half days to see you. I'm not going

to waste a moment. If I'm lucky, maybe I can negotiate one more day with the officers." Eddie pouted.

Amanda bit her cheek, trying to contain her laughter at his childlike expression.

"Eddie, I love you, but I need you in top form before my parents come back. Dad is a little bit of a stickler."

She swallowed. *I love him. I really do. Does he feel the same? Should I ask him? No, he'll inform me when the time is right. It's not something I can rush. He doesn't have to tell me. I can love enough for both of us.*

Eddie stayed quiet. Had he heard her say she loved him? He looked down at the ground and slowly moved off the bed and picked up his shoes. He turned his gaze to her. His eyes sparkled like the brightest of stars on the darkest of nights. The corners of his eyes were wet with tears threatening to fall. Their heavy breathing filled the silence. He swallowed hard.

His eyes tell me everything I need to know.

Eddie sat in the chair next to Amanda and put his shoes back on. His expression turned into a smirk. "Speaking of your father… I've already met the man. We have an understanding between one another."

Amanda cocked her head to the side. Her curls fell over her eyes. "Huh. What did you have to promise them?" She fought the urge to cross her arms.

Eddie shrugged. "They were pretty easygoing. But if you're asking, I offered to introduce them to my parents and give them a tour of Buckingham Palace. I was thinking of asking David to fill in for me, though. I need to be here with you."

"So in other words, you're going to pawn them off on David so you can monopolize me."

Eddie winced. "When you put it that way…" His cheeks colored.

"I approve," Amanda said gleefully. "I'll just tell my dad

that his little princess has requested to spend all her time with her prince. I have him wrapped around my finger."

They laughed. Eddie had drastically improved her spirits. She felt hopeful and almost back to her old self. She had missed his banter and the intimate moments they shared. He was an extension of herself.

Amanda winced. "Ow. Head. Ribs."

Eddie stood, stretched his neck from side to side, and brushed invisible dirt off of his trousers. He pressed his lips against Amanda's cheek in a soft kiss. "I'll be back this afternoon to see you," he whispered.

The door to the room opened and broke the spell. Clara entered, feigning offense. "I see I'm not the only visitor today, A. You had a nurse text me SOS. If I had known Eddie was coming so early, I would've stayed at the studio for the afternoon."

"C! About time you got here too! Eddie was just heading out to shower and shave. Can you help me get myself together? I need some makeup assistance, per favore!" Amanda exclaimed to her bestie before turning to Eddie. "Gotta look my best for when you return and take me home for our date tonight."

"Enjoy your girl time. I'll be back as soon as I see my father and change, Collins. Be prepared. Have Clara text me if you would like me to come back with any special food requests. I just got my mobile back, and I'll be stopping by Waitrose on my way home." Eddie winked and left the room.

Amanda felt a pang of disappointment as she watched him go. She needed to maintain a semblance of normalcy. The last thing she wanted was for Clara to baby her. She put on a smile for her friend.

"Putting me to work already, A. All right. I just want to eat my bento box first. And I have some fun news for you! David and I have decided to get a puppy. We're still in negotiations about the breed. There are so many people to appease. Who would have known?"

Amanda's thoughts wandered. "C, I forgot to ask. Am I able to stay at your place while I recover? I don't want to impose on you and David."

Clara stopped eating and frowned at her. "Of course you're staying with us! Did you really think I was going to leave you on your own? No. No. No. No. No."

Amanda snorted. That was one problem sorted.

Chapter Twenty-Five

EDDIE

O f all of the rooms in Buckingham Palace, his father's office was one of Eddie's favorites. The walls were lined with decorations and ornaments collected over generations. A small fire crackled, warming the room.

Eddie yawned, the comforting heat of the room lulling him into sleepiness.

This is how I'll become addicted to coffee. Amanda will never believe I'm becoming an early riser without seeing it. The blokes still give me a hard time about my ability to sleep like the dead. I swear I'm getting better at being more aware of my surroundings.

In front of the fire, the family's English springer spaniel, Francine aka Franny, was curled up, fast asleep. If there was ever a spoiled pet, it was Franny. Her chocolate and white markings and big droopy brown eyes were something nobody in the family could resist.

Eddie leaned over to greet his old friend, giving her a good scratch behind her ears as she happily rolled over onto her back for a belly rub. He indulged her for a few moments, watching as she opened her eyes, gave his hand a friendly lick, then went back to sleep.

The office door swung open, and Eddie's father entered. He immediately straightened up, adopting a poised and alert posture. In private, the royal family normally dispensed with the formalities and bows, but this was different. Eddie was now an army recruit, and his father was the head of the armed forces.

"Trooper Wales, reporting as ordered, sir." He saluted.

The king chuckled and performed a mock officer's inspection.

"At ease, Trooper Wales. Come here." His father clapped him on the back in a half hug. "Army life agrees with you. I'm so proud of the efforts you've been putting in. I have it on good authority that you're on your way to becoming one of the top recruits in your class. Well done, indeed."

He puffed his chest out. "Sir, I've been working hard to make the family proud. The chaps in my group have been easy to train with."

For the most part. It sounds like Dad is in a good mood. It couldn't hurt to ask for that extra day of leave.

Eddie cleared his throat. "Father, would you be able to possibly sort out an extra day of leave for me?"

"And the reason?"

"To spend more time with my girlfriend—" Eddie was stopped before he could go any further.

"Edmund, if I were your commanding officer, what do you think the answer would be?"

"No."

"There's your answer."

The king took a seat on the sofa across from the fireplace and gestured for Eddie to join him. When his father wanted to sit on his couch, it meant a serious discussion. He sighed and sat down.

"Edmund, I understand the desire to be with Miss Collins, especially given recent events. However, you're chosen a path of military service. As the Prince of Wales, any decision you make reflects not just on you as an individual, but also on the royal family as a whole," the king advised in a measured tone.

Eddie nodded, absorbing the gravity of his father's words.

"I'm not denying the importance of personal relationships," he added. "I'm just here to advise you that you will need to figure out the right balance between your duty to the crown and the country and your responsibilities to those you care about."

I'm the Prince of Wales. If I get an extra day of leave to be with Amanda, it would be given to me because of who I am. If I were any other recruit, the leave would only be granted if it were a true emergency.

Amanda is technically on the road to recovery. One of the reasons I enlisted in the first place was to negate the idea that I was receiving any special treatment. I understand now.

For the first time, Eddie began to realize the complexity of his situation. "Father… if you were in my shoes, what would you do?"

"If I were you, son, I'd have an open conversation with Miss Collins, so she understands the demands that are being asked of you. From what I've heard from David, she has a good head on her shoulders." The king stood and poured two glasses of port from the crystal decanter on the side table. "After all, the keys to any successful relationship are communication and understanding."

"Amanda is unlike any other woman I've ever dated," Eddie admitted, accepting the glass from his father. "Even when she was in the hospital, I instinctually knew that if I went to see her before I was granted leave, she'd be cross with me." He stared at the amber-colored liquid. "I know she won't have any problems understanding what's going on. But that doesn't stop me from feeling guilty."

"Unfortunately, it never gets any easier." His father crossed one leg over the other. "I'll admit I was genuinely surprised to learn from Jonathan that you were in a relationship, and it was serious."

"Neither Amanda nor I wanted to rush into a relationship as I have in the past. We became friends when David began dating Clara. Over the last few months, our friendship has grown, and we both knew that dating was the natural next step." Eddie's cheeks warmed. "I wasn't ready to say anything to you or Mum. I guess I wanted what I have with Amanda to stay between us as long as possible. I didn't want to share her with anyone else."

"I understand," his father said.

Franny stirred, making her way over to the king's feet, hopeful for a treat. He sighed and pulled one from his trouser pocket. "You're too smart for your own good, Franny," he teased the dog. "I hope you'll bring Miss Collins around for tea when she's feeling better. I'd like to meet her."

"I will."

He paused as a servant knocked, entered the room, and brought in a tea service. The king thanked and dismissed the servant. "Are we expecting Mother to join us?" Eddie raised his eyebrow.

The king's face flashed briefly, showing a slip of sadness before returning to his usual composure. "Your mother has a charity engagement that couldn't be cleared from her diary. She sends her regrets." He sighed and turned to gaze at the photos on his desk, a faraway look in his eyes.

"I think it's fair to tell you that your mother and I have been going through a rough patch. You may find us needing more space from one another than usual," he admitted, leaving it at that.

Eddie tensed. He knew better than to pry. "Do you think Mother would be willing to meet Amanda?"

As he grew older, Eddie was beginning to understand that his parents may not have been as happily settled as he had always pictured. They had married young, prompted by Eddie's grandmother, the late queen. They shared few interests, leading him to always wonder how they had been married for over twenty years. Perhaps he had his answer now.

"I'm certain she would," his father said in a neutral tone. "No matter what may be going on between us, you and Alice are our children. We both love you and want to see you two happy, no matter what."

Suddenly, something David said a few days ago caused him to freeze. Carefully, he asked, "Mum's not happy about David choosing to marry an American, is she?"

Father's silence spoke volumes. His Adam's apple bobbed up and down. "She'll come around in time. David is happy and that's all that matters."

Eddie felt hurt, but not surprised. He had long understood his mother's expectations regarding whom he should marry. To him, that aspect of his future always felt distant. Until now, there had never been any thoughts of settling down or having a long-term relationship. Being in the army and seeing the burgeoning relationship between David and Clara offered him a new perspective.

When he was with Amanda, he felt valued for being Eddie the man and not the title. He loved the way she encouraged him to constantly step out of his comfort zone. He yearned for adventures and to heartedly laugh out loud at the world around him. Being a prince, he would always live in a bubble, but with Amanda around, being in the bubble wasn't so bad.

He released his hold of the couch cushion he was gripping hard.

I'll make Mum understand just how important Amanda is to me. I don't care what her opinions are. It's my life.

With those thoughts, Eddie felt free. Forget expectations. In the end, he wanted to be happy.

"Edmund?" His father had a hint of worry in his voice. "Don't let your mind dwell on your mother and me. Everything will sort itself out." The king stood and finished off his glass of port. "I invited David to join us for a quick word. I have some news for you two, then I'll send you off. I know you wish to maximize your time with Miss Collins."

Eddie set to work pouring three teacups and helped himself to a sandwich. He waited for directions from his father, who told him, "Go ahead and help yourself."

I do need to sleep and clean myself up. Amanda was right. I need a nap before I return to the hospital today.

A knock interrupted his musings. "Enter!" the king bellowed. Once a military man, always a military man. "Ah, David. Perfect timing. What's the update?"

David entered the room and immediately noticed Eddie's choice of footwear. He raised an eyebrow. "Nice shoes, cousin." His voice dripped with sarcasm.

Eddie frowned and glanced down at his feet, realizing his mistake. He groaned to himself. He had two different style shoes—one black and one brown. Why hadn't he noticed it earlier? Leave it to his shoe-making cousin to take note. Eddie signaled for him to take a seat next to him, choosing not to respond.

"I have some news that should interest you, Eddie. Firstly, everything is set for our artist gala. My mum has agreed to take on the role of hostess for the evening. She claims that it's the perfect opportunity try out some of her food ideas for my wedding."

David and Eddie exchanged a knowing look. Both were

aware of Princess Charlotte's deep, obsessive involvement in the planning of David and Clara's upcoming wedding.

"Typical Lottie, tying everything back to the wedding," remarked the king as he stood up, offering refreshments to his nephew. "Sorry for the interruption. Please continue, David. What is your second piece of news?"

David finished chewing a bite of his sandwich and continued. "Clara just rang me from the hospital. Amanda is ready to be discharged. We've arranged to have her brought over to our Kensington flat."

Perfect. That's right next to my flat.

"Her parents will be returning to America tomorrow evening, once she's settled. Dr. Evans will continue to oversee her recovery. It's going to be a while before she's completely free of concussion symptoms. There's a pretty detailed list of what she can and can't do."

Clara or David can fill me in later. Amanda is going to get bored quickly. How are we going to entertain her for a couple of weeks?

Eddie took a moment to rest his eyes, temporarily tuning out David and his father. He envisioned himself sitting on David and Clara's oversized sofa, cradling Amanda in his arms and playfully twirling the ends of her hair as they debated their favorite Disney villains.

"Eddie?"

"Huh?" He turned his head and looked at David. "I'm sorry, what was that again?"

David raised an eyebrow. "I was just telling Uncle Reg that Mr. and Mrs. Collins have agreed to have dinner with you and your parents tonight."

"And I mentioned to David that I'd ask your mother to join us," the king added.

Eddie's hand flew to his forehead. "Dinner... I'd forgotten

I'd asked you to make arrangements, David!" He turned to his father. "I'm sorry, Dad, I thought that maybe… if you had time in your schedule… it would be nice if…"

His father held up his hand. "Edmund, you don't have to explain. I understand and I think it's an excellent idea"—he winked—"but perhaps it would be best for you if it was just us older parents."

He covered a yawn with his hand. His eyelids were getting heavy. "Are you certain?"

"Yes, son. I am."

"Thank you."

David draped his arm over Eddie's shoulder. "Come on, then, off we go. You can take a nap on my sofa if you can't make it to your place. I'll wake you when Amanda gets released."

Eddie perked up. "I only live next door to you! I can manage the journey. What I really need is a clean bed and no more horse-related responsibilities."

The king and David exchanged looks, knowing full well how great a non-military-issued bed felt on an exhausted body.

"Edmund, take care of yourself," his father said kindly, then he snapped his fingers. "There is one last bit of news before I forget—Franny is due to have another litter of puppies."

Eddie swallowed hard. "Can I have one?"

Maybe a puppy would be just the thing to keep Amanda company.

David burst out laughing. "Really, Eddie? When do you have time to care for a puppy?"

"For Amanda." He gritted his teeth.

I understand I don't have time to care for one.

"Of course, Edmund, but it'll be several weeks before the puppies arrive. After they're weaned, you may take your pick from the litter. I'll leave you two to see yourselves out. I have a meeting to take with the prime minister."

Glancing at the mantel clock, the king nodded to his son and nephew before making his way toward his library, which doubled as a receiving area.

David guided Eddie toward the waiting car out front. On the ride home, he reflected more thoroughly on his relationship with Amanda.

He had frozen when she told him she loved him earlier that day. How could he have been so cowardly as to not be able to say "I love you" in return?

I've never told any woman outside my family that I love them. I've never cared about anyone the way that I do about Amanda. I hope she doesn't interpret my silence as a sign that I don't care. I should ring her. Oh wait, she won't be able to answer her phone. I'll tell her in person.

He stifled a yawn, the steady hum of the car's engine causing his body to relax. His breathing began to even out as he rested his head against the window for a moment.

"Eddie?" David asked.

"Hmm?" He opened his tired eyes and focused on his cousin.

"You're thinking about her, aren't you?" David wore a bemused grin that Eddie wished he could wipe off. He supposed it was payback for all the times he had given his cousin a difficult time.

"Yeah, I am. I'm just wondering where I'm going to go from here."

"A film and Chinese food?" David's words reinvigorated Eddie.

"Ordering takeaway is a brilliant idea, but I promised Amanda that I'd cook for her. Maybe I could pretend I cooked it? No, Amanda is too smart... she'll see right through the charade." He sighed. "Could I borrow a few ingredients from you and Clara? My chef has been reassigned to Buckingham Palace. I'm sure my kitchen is empty." Eddie glanced at his watch and cursed himself.

"Whatever you need, Eddie. Sleep. I'll wake you later."

Chapter Twenty-Six

AMANDA

Amanda, unable to dance in the seat of her wheelchair, tapped her fingers with boundless amounts of energy in the hospital's reception area. The Beach Boys tune "California Girls" played inside her head. She sang the chorus out loud and pretended to hit an invisible drum set with her good arm.

It wasn't going too smoothly, with the heavy cast on her right arm severely limiting all her movement, but she managed. The people around her in the waiting room watched with amusement, her actions bringing smiles to a few faces. Others stared as if she were a bit eccentric.

I can't wait for some quality time with Princey!

Was he on his way? Amanda wondered what time it was. She stared longingly at the empty wheelchair next to her and the long hallway off to the side. She could picture herself racing down the hall against Eddie.

I bet we could wrangle some of his security team officers into letting us do it. After all, wheelchairs are much safer than race cars.

Amanda glanced down at her incapacitated arm, feeling a sudden wave of doubt and anxiety. Would she ever recover?

I won't be able to do anything without help. She had felt so good after Clara's assistance with doing her hair and makeup—more put together. *I need to draw on those same feelings from earlier.*

"Oy! You aren't allowed in here. Get out!" Amanda heard a commotion unfolding near the hospital's entrance doors.

A hospital security guard seemed to be grappling with someone holding a camera. Bright flashes brought on a sudden wave of dizziness. Her headache worsened.

Her chair was swiftly maneuvered out of the reception area and down the hall opposite where her room had been. Glancing around, she noticed the commotion had captured the attention of those in the waiting area. They were unaware of her being wheeled away.

"Ms. Collins, put these sunglasses on. It should help with the bright lights," a winded male voice instructed her.

A pair of oversized aviators were pressed into her hand. Amanda tried to look over her shoulder, but the abrupt stop-and-start motions and jerking of the chair made her stomach uncomfortably unsettled, inducing nausea. The flashes persisted around her. She wasted no time putting the sunglasses on.

"What's happening? Who are you? Where are we going? Are you some kind of MI-5 spy? Are you 007?" she inquired, feeling uncertain about the man maneuvering her through the hospital.

They changed directions twice. *Does this dude even know where he's going? Should I trust him?* The Bond theme song began playing in her mind. *Dum-dum-da-dum-da-do-dah. I really need to stop with the theme music.*

"My name is Michael. I am the Duke of Leeds's chauffeur. The Prince of Wales was to meant be your escort until we entered the hospital's car park. We're having your parents exit through a different area of the hospital to divert attention. The press has caught wind of your connection to the royal family. We suspect it might have been an intern. I'm sorry if I'm moving too quickly," Michael said.

Amanda realized she was in trouble. She swallowed hard. *Not like this wasn't going to happen eventually.*

"Normally I wouldn't trust a stranger I just met, but I do know your name. Our pal Leeds has mentioned you a few times. You're one of the good guys, but it sounds like you got the short end of the stick today."

She took several breaths, hoping it would assist with the nausea. "We're going underground now, aren't we? If I were to film this, I'd have the car pull up hastily the moment we get down to the garage. I'd radio ahead and have Princey swoop in to save the day."

Michael slowed his pace and chuckled. "I've heard you were spirited. Yes, we're heading to the underground car park. Actually, your assessment is fairly accurate. I had to phone over to the Wales security team to bring in some extra assistance."

Michael stopped, and just as Amanda had predicted, a black Range Rover with tinted windows pulled up at the same time they reached the lowest level of the hospital. He opened the car door and assisted her in getting into the car.

She was still a little dizzy after the frantic race down to the basement, but was determined to walk under her own power. In the back seat, patiently waiting for her, was Eddie. Amanda drank in the sight of her prince. He didn't appear to be in a good mood.

"Lousy press. If I had it my way, I'd give them a piece of my mind and let them know *exactly* how angry I am right now. You're off-limits. It's a complete and utter invasion of your privacy to hold vigil outside a hospital, for goodness' sake. If I ever find out who tipped them off, they'll be at the receiving end of my fist."

Eddie was sexy when he was in a mood. Amanda eyed his pumped-up, tense muscles. The suit jacket was off, tie gone, and his shirt was ruffled and unbuttoned at the top. Did he notice his suit and shoes were both mismatched?

"I kind of like it when you're angry. You're so saucy. Nice suit, by the way." Amanda brushed her lips on his cheek in an attempt to ease his agitation. He tasted salty, but his cheek was smooth from a recent shave. He had fulfilled one of her two requests. Had he napped too? "Mind helping a girl with her seat belt?" She inclined her head.

"I'm sorry, Collins. I'm distracted. What's wrong with my suit? David mentioned the shoes, not the suit," Eddie responded, looking momentarily confused.

He looks so masculine… like a young James Bond.

Not two seconds later, with the wheelchair stowed in the trunk of the car, the Range Rover sped away.

"Your suit jacket is a slightly different shade than the trousers." Eddie glanced down at his ensemble, and his cheeks colored.

"Jon. He's colorblind. Last time I let him pick out my suit, shoes, and tie," he grumbled.

"I like it. It's very me. So, my parents? Where are they being taken? Did you manage to arrange some time for us tonight? I didn't get to touch base with them. David said they were caught up at Harrods. Dad is probably going crazy figuring out all the extra luggage he's going to have to buy to get Mom's purchases home."

The car jerked suddenly. Amanda's injured arm collided with the side of the car. Her face paled. *Count backward from ten.* She made a fist. Eddie grabbed her, pulling her close and using his body as a human shield to protect her from any further jolts.

The pain gradually subsided into a constant throb after about a minute. "My deepest apologies, Ms. Collins. I am doing my best to evade the paparazzi following us on mopeds," Michael explained, keeping his eyes firmly focused on the road.

Navigating through the many cars on the streets between central London and Kensington Palace proved somewhat difficult. Traffic around the city could be wildly unpredictable.

"S'all right," she breathed.

"It's not all right. Look at what they've done now! If they caused you to reinjure your arm…" Eddie trailed off.

He ran his hands over Amanda's cast. She buried her head into his chest, listening to the comforting sound of his heartbeat. The soft linen of his shirt served as a makeshift pillow against her bruises. Another bright flash through the window of the back seat caused Eddie to curse and use his jacket to block any unwanted light from entering the vehicle.

"Nothing we can do about it. Now distract me. What are my parents up to?" Amanda sucked in another breath as she repositioned herself, burrowing deeper into him.

"Right, your parents. They're having dinner with my mum and dad at Windsor. My father said we're excused. He wanted us to spend some time together. Do you think they'll get along?"

"Yes. My mom can strike up a conversation with just about anyone. Daddy usually finds it a bit tougher, but I'm sure he'll manage. I just hope they don't exchange any embarrassing stories about us."

"You and me both." Eddie kissed the top of her head. "I bet you were a perfect child growing up."

"Far from it. Believe it or not, I was a total tomboy. I used to dress in Dad's old airline uniforms and strut around the house in them. Between the ages of about eight to ten, pretty much every photo my mom took of me featured me in an oversized white shirt, Dad's hat and tie, and aviator sunglasses."

He drew circles on her back. "I'm surprised you didn't become a pilot."

"I thought about it as a teen, but Dad discouraged it. He and Mom wanted me to have a *normal* job, in their words, but being normal isn't for me."

"I wouldn't have it any other way, Collins."

<h1>Chapter Twenty-Seven</h1>

AMANDA

The Range Rover eventually reached the private entrance to Kensington Palace. They drove up the lengthy gravel driveway to the twin entrances to apartments 1A and 1B, where Eddie, David, and Clara resided. Amanda wasn't too confident of her ability to maneuver the stairs after the rough car ride over.

Taking matters into his own hands, Eddie carried her up the steps to his cousin's apartment. He moved carefully and deliberately as they passed through the black-and-white checkered entryway and straight to the ground floor guest suite. Amanda nestled her head against Eddie's chest, appreciating the feel of his muscles and the scent of his lemon and sandalwood cologne. Her insides tingled with delight, cherishing this intimate moment.

Once they were inside, they found Dr. Evans was ready to conduct another medical examination on Amanda's arm and ribs. After rewrapping her ribs and assessing her condition, he advised her to rest, emphasizing that sleep was her best medicine. Dr. Evans didn't linger long, but promised to return soon for a follow-up.

After the excitement of the afternoon, Amanda was eager to settle in and enjoy the comfort of being at home. For now, her temporary dwelling was the ground floor guest suite of David's apartment. The word apartment, however, was an understatement.

Amanda's entire Irvine apartment, consisting of two bedrooms, a kitchen, living room, and bathroom, could easily fit within just one of the en suite rooms on the ground floor! The scale of the residence was staggering, boasting a total of about fifteen rooms.

Everywhere she looked, she noticed Clara's influence on the flat's decor, including vases brimming with freshly arranged flowers and a few coffee table books from her previous home in LA. She had artfully transformed and elevated much of David's bachelor pad into a space that could grace the pages of a home design magazine. Blending the historical charm of Kensington Palace with a twist in decor was a challenging task, but Clara had managed it with finesse.

For now, all Amanda wanted was to unwind and spend some quality time on the pullout sectional with her boyfriend. They both agreed that the sofa would be the most comfortable place to sleep upright.

"This is the life." Amanda sighed happily, closing her eyes and sinking into the plush cushions.

Eddie carefully placed a pillow under her arm to provide support for her cast. She opened her eyes as he sat beside her, gently turning her body toward his. He had her stretch out so her head could rest on his lap.

He started massaging Amanda's neck and head. "Let me show you how to truly relax."

She groaned in delight. "That feels soooooooooo gooooooood." Eddie's hands worked on the tense spots around her shoulder, and she melted into his touch. She'd waited all day to be in his intoxicating presence. In the car, she had felt so vulnerable.

She'd never experienced such limited mobility in her body. The adrenaline had kept her going earlier, but now, within the comfort of her own "home," she felt safe. Eddie's thoughtful act of relieving her stress and tension made her feel incredibly loved.

"How do you know where to maaaaaaaaaaaassage?" He had pinpointed one of the trigger points on her left side near her shoulder.

He chuckled. "Growing up playing polo, I've taken my fair share of falls off horses. Over the years, I've learned where my body feels the most tense. Your poor battered body felt so stiff in my arms. I suspected the areas I usually need to be worked on were the same as yours."

Eddie paused and carefully moved closer to her. Licking his lips, he met her in a caress of his mouth against hers. They formed the perfect unit, only to be interrupted by her growling stomach.

He laughed. Amanda's face, still warm from his kiss, now burned. "I hate to interrupt this love fest, but this girl's stomach has a plan of its own, especially now that I can have real food and not the hospital stuff." She patted her stomach.

Eddie stood. "Originally, I'd planned to cook for you, but with all the craziness of earlier, we'll have to settle for takeaway."

His demeanor had shifted to playful and relaxed now that they were safely inside the walls of Kensington Palace.

"Did you put your mad takeaway ordering skills to the test?" Amanda asked.

"Not this time. I was told by a certain somebody to take a nap, so I asked David to do the honors," he replied, assisting her into an upright position. He then made his way to the kitchenette just off the living room.

Eddie skimmed a note from David taped to the mini refrigerator, opened it, and pulled out seven containers.

He opened each one and rolled his eyes. "We have a strange mixture of Chinese, Thai, and Italian dishes to choose from. My cousin couldn't seem to decide what you'd like and ordered some of everything. Clara wouldn't have ordered so many uncomplementary dishes."

"So long as there's dessert involved, I'll happily try some of everything, please," Amanda called over.

Eddie made a face of mock disgust at her food choices, prompting her to burst into laughter. Grabbing clean plates, utensils, and glasses, he took on the role of waiter and began warming up the containers in the microwave.

"If you wouldn't mind setting up the entertainment system, I'd like us to watch some episodes of *I Love Lucy* tonight," Amanda said, not wanting to leave the comfort of the couch. "I'm not supposed to watch the screen, but if you could put the volume on low, I'd love to listen to the audio and have you sit with me.

"In my bag of goodies from Mom, there's a collection of my favorite 'sick day' DVDs straight from home. I haven't watched some of them in years. Do you have a favorite Lucy episode?" she asked.

The delectable aroma of food filled the air. Eddie presented a well-arranged plate with curry, spaghetti, sushi, and rice. *That smells so good!*

"Is Lucy an American actress?" he asked as he handed Amanda her plate and dutifully set up the television and DVD player for her.

How was she going to do this? She would have to sit facing backward, away from the screen. Fortunately, she'd seen every episode a few thousand times and could easily conjure up each scene in her mind.

"How have you never seen an episode of *I Love Lucy*?"

Amanda asked incredulously. "Actually, I should be asking you how you've never heard of Lucille Ball. She's a legend!"

As she went through her collection, contemplating which episode to watch, Eddie responded with a nonchalant shrug, serving himself some Italian food and leaving the rest for her.

He set his plate on the table next to her food.

"Enough stalling. Let's dive in to my favorite comedian. I predict that by the end of the next few hours, you'll be hooked. Don't look at me with a sour face. You'll be thanking me." Amanda said, grinning, while Eddie pouted.

She flipped back and forth through the label of episodes on her DVDs. *I'd better find a good one to start with. Oh, I'm definitely starting with Lucy and Ethel getting jobs in the chocolate factory. Then again, vitameatavegamin is a good one too. No, chocolate factory first.*

Eddie stood with arms crossed, waiting for Amanda to hand him a DVD. "I'm afraid of what you're about to get me into. I haven't had access to a telly in weeks. This is a right welcome treat for me, especially since it doesn't involve horses and cleaning up after them."

That was an understatement. Eddie could easily get addicted to anything, as Amanda had come to find out when first introducing him to the '90s American sitcoms *Family Matters* and *Home Improvement*. They had quickly added *Doctor Who* and *Sherlock* to their repertoire for their virtual dates over video chat.

She carefully handed her chosen disk to Eddie, who popped it into David and Clara's DVD player.

He stopped short of turning the television on. "I forgot. You aren't allowed to watch any screens or read. We can't watch this."

Amanda laughed. "I told you, I've already gotten that figured out. All we have to do is turn the sound as low as you can and have me sit facing backward or with an eye mask."

Eddie rolled his eyes and moved the heavy gray recliner from the far side of the room, situating it next to the sofa. Amanda admired his muscles at work under his white dress shirt and the thin sheen of perspiration on his brow from the exertion.

After a moment's effort, he caught his breath. She gingerly scooted forward and made her way over to the recliner, Eddie hovering attentively, ready to assist her at a moment's notice.

Amanda settled into the recliner as he fetched a cushion from the sofa, arranging it to support her arm. Her stomach growled again. He observed the situation with a hint of amusement. She glanced longingly over at the coffee table.

"Out of curiosity, just how do you propose to be able to eat your dinner in the chair with one arm? Were you going to balance your dinner on your cast?" Eddie asked.

The realization struck her—this might be decidedly more challenging than she had imagined. Her cheeks colored.

"Welp, since you're on Amanda-sitting duty, this is embarrassing, but I might need some help feeding myself," she admitted.

Eddie hesitated momentarily. "I know it's difficult to ask for help, but I'm here for you. I'll do anything you need."

Amanda chewed on her lip. "It doesn't feel right to interrupt your dinner."

Eddie ran his hand through his hair. "I'll eat while I watch *Lucy* and you listen to it."

He went over to the table, grabbed Amanda's plate, and brought it over to the recliner. She adjusted the leg rest, and he slowly settled into the chair. It supported his weight with no issues. Their eyes met. An electric spark jolted between the two of them. "Thank you for everything, Princey. Truly," she whispered.

Eddie took up a small forkful of spaghetti. His eyes twinkled as he fed her. "You're my girl."

To Amanda's surprise, they managed with relatively little mess. After she finished, Eddie reheated his own dinner and found a spot on the sofa nearest her. He turned the television on, lowered the volume as much as possible, and selected the first episode on the list.

"Be prepared to be amazed," Amanda said, motioning for Eddie to start the show. The opening theme song played, and she closed her eyes, reveling in the quiet and familiar lull.

"It's in black and white? Just how old is this show?" Eddie asked in shock.

Amanda chuckled. "It's a classic of the 1950s. Don't judge until you've seen at least three episodes. The beauty is you don't have to see them in order to appreciate Lucy's comedic genius. Stop me if my quoting every episode gets to be too much. On second thought, pause the DVD really quick."

Amanda turned her head to Eddie and fought the instinct to look over to the TV. "So I'll give you the basics, so you're not completely lost. The show centers on two couples, Lucy and Ricky Ricardo and Fred and Ethel Mertz. They live in New York, where the Mertzes own the apartment building that the Ricardos live in. They're best friends. Ricky is a Cuban bandleader and Lucy is always trying to get into show business and into Ricky's act."

"Sounds like fun." Amanda caught Eddie's sarcasm and gave him a glare.

"Don't knock it until you've tried it, as I always say. Have I ever steered you wrong?" She returned to her spot and lay back. "Here we go." Eddie unpaused the episode as she quoted the opening lines.

Chapter Twenty-Eight

EDDIE

Amanda was fast asleep not too far into the fifth episode. Eddie congratulated himself on not bombarding her with too many questions. As usual, she had been right—*Lucy* was indeed addicting. Maybe he could play the song "Babalou" for her on the piano.

He envisioned her delight and pearly-white smile when the notes filled the room, but his thoughts were interrupted by Clara's voice, whispering from the doorway. "You know, Amanda's dream date is going to a nightclub and dancing the jitterbug, just like the *Lucy* episode where she learns how to do it from King Cat Walsh."

Eddie's gaze shifted to Clara, who still had stage makeup on her face and was dressed in a Westminster Ballet tracksuit. He yawned and glanced at the Rolex watch on his left wrist— it was past midnight.

"I just poked my head in to see how you guys were getting on. David's out like a light," she said, motioning for him to join her outside the room.

Eddie checked on Amanda. She was miraculously still

sitting upright in her chair. He tucked her in, tiptoed out of the room into the hallway, and silently closed the door.

"You're beginning to sound like a proper Brit," he whispered back, a hint of amusement in his voice. "I have no idea who King Cat Walsh is, but I'll find out soon enough. I have a feeling some dancing lessons are in my future. It's a good thing I have access to such an esteemed dancer."

"You're really good for my bestie, you know. You've matured a lot in the last couple of months, Eddie. I'm proud of you." Clara hugged him.

He basked in the glow of the compliment. He had come to greatly value Clara's opinion and friendship over the last few months. It meant a lot to him for her to see how much he had grown.

"I'm heading up to bed as soon as I wash my face. Help yourself to anything you need."

"Thanks, Clara. Good night."

After she ascended the stairs, Eddie headed off to raid the kitchen on the first floor of the flat. He was still hungry, and he knew David and Clara could be counted on to provide him with snacks. When Eddie was younger, David would keep a hidden drawer of treats for him in his office. As an adult, he had been upgraded to an entire cabinet.

In his stockinged feet, Eddie padded up the stairs to the kitchen and opened the mahogany door. He scanned the shelves.

Someone noticed I was low on chocolate and jerky and restocked it. Brilliant. Eddie's hands went to the beef jerky and almonds. *On second thought, I'll come back for these. Amanda is going to need her meds and water when she wakes up.*

Closing the cabinet, he fought off another yawn and descended the stairs back to the ground floor to prepare things for Amanda in the morning before leaving for his own home.

Chapter Twenty-Nine

EDDIE

The formal dining room wasn't often used. Before Clara's renovation efforts, it had been dark, dated, and smelled of damp. However, after a fresh coat of paint, new furniture, and updated decor, the room was transformed into a light, airy space. It was the perfect room for a breakfast gathering.

On the round mahogany table, an array of fresh seasonal fruit, granola, meats, waffles, coffee, juice, and tea were meticulously arranged. Clara added the final touches, placing containers of fresh, hot maple syrup and butter on the table as Amanda, Eddie, and David looked on.

"Not bad, C. Even the flowers in the vase are fresh. Not sure when you popped off to the grocery store, but you've outdone yourself. You're learning how to cook. I'm impressed," Amanda gushed.

"David's been a wonderful teacher."

"You're the ideal student." David beamed at his soon-to-be bride. "This looks positively scrumptious. Thank you for the excellent spread, Clare-bear."

Eddie couldn't help but hope he might be as fortunate as

his cousin one day in winning Amanda's heart. The way David looked at Clara in adoration made it clear to all just how deeply he loved her.

Mr. and Mrs. Collins, whose departure plans had suddenly changed, skimmed over the headlines of assorted papers on the table with somewhat grim expressions. Instead of focusing on Eddie, no less than four tabloid headlines centered upon Amanda's hasty retreat from the hospital.

"'The American Invasion,' 'The Heir's New Spare,' 'Is the Yankee Fit for Duty?' These headlines aren't even that imaginative. I hate the way I look in this photo. I'm all swollen and bruised," Amanda remarked, squinting at her hair flying in every direction in the tabloid's photo. "My makeup is on point. Have to hand it to you, C."

Eddie's reaction was markedly different. He grimaced at Amanda's reading of the papers. "This is an unacceptable way to photograph you. You were leaving the hospital, for pity's sake," he fumed, clenching his fists and feeling the heat of anger rise within him.

Amanda is my girlfriend. I love her too much to let the press get to her. This is only the beginning. Life as we know it changes from here. I want her to be protected. I want her to have a life and not live under a microscope.

Could she cope with the pressure? Eddie had been born into this life. What was her choice going to be? Did she want all that being a royal entailed?

"We've touched on this before, Princey. The media is going to do what they are going to do. You take the tabloids with a grain of salt."

Eddie remained rigid. How could she be so nonchalant? Did she truly not care that much? What about the useless rubbish and riffraff that were going to hound her and follow her every move?

"Amanda is right. You two have had maybe four or five

months of privacy now. Didn't you yourself say you've been lucky each time the two of you have met up? I understand you may be upset, Eddie, but consider taking control of the situation," Clara suggested.

"I spoke with the press office this morning," David added. "They want you two to issue a statement now, so we can control what gets out and what you want the public to know. They may be more sympathetic to you that way."

Clara signaled for everyone to help themselves to breakfast. Mrs. Collins took on the role of assisting her daughter with feeding herself. Eddie's demeanor softened watching Amanda. She looked so innocent and helpless.

How dare anyone mess with my woman.

He couldn't shake the concern from his mind no matter what was said to him.

Amanda sipped some coffee before diving into her waffles. "I have to admit, this is a lot for anyone to handle. I wanted to keep everything a secret as long as possible. But time's up. This is the price I pay for having an amazing boyfriend. I'll do whatever it takes to be with him. Eddie, I need to hear your thoughts. I have nothing to hide. That's why I closed off all my social media accounts."

He ran a hand through his closely cropped hair. Even six weeks into his cavalry course, he still wasn't used to having it so short.

"You shouldn't have to give up anything for anyone, Collins. However, the most pressing matter is your safety. The motorbike member of the paparazzo is just the tip of the iceberg. The gauntlet will drop the moment we are confirmed to be a couple. The scope of everything officially changes from this point forward. I've always been more of a target than someone like David." Eddie winced at the memory of his partying days. "There are a few factors to consider."

Clara nudged him and handed him a plate heaping with

food. "Since you won't help yourself," she emphasized. Food was the way of changing Eddie from angry to grumpy. He inhaled the scent of the fresh maple syrup and poked his fork at the crisp golden-brown edges and took a bite.

Mr. Collins leaned back in his chair and crossed his arms. "Edmund here has brought up my number-one concern, Leeds. I hope you have some ideas. My daughter's safety is also my priority. To the rubbish bin with the press, as my wife says. When we heard Amanda was dating you, I was all riled up and prepared to talk her out of it. She is stubborn, but I also want her to be happy. Anyone can see that she's crazy about you, so I'll do whatever it takes. She won't change her mind. If I have to, I'll move here and personally guard my daughter to ensure they don't get within twenty feet of my Amanda."

Amanda paused and gave her father a one-armed hug from where she was seated. "Thank you, Daddy." She flashed him a million-watt smile.

Then she turned her head to Eddie. Looking up from his plate between bites, he observed the nondescript smiles Amanda shot at him. What had he been so worried about? He was an idiot for having other thoughts. Of course Amanda would be her own woman and do what she set her mind to.

David pushed his plate aside. "I rang my uncle, who mentioned there is not much we can do as of yet. Clara is entitled to a security team as a future member of the family. Amanda is not. She is still considered a private citizen."

Eddie froze from his waffle midbite.

David cleaned his face with a napkin. "Don't worry. I have a couple of ideas to address the security problem."

Eddie relaxed and resumed eating.

"Good. I'm not leaving the UK until we get this settled. Let's hear what you've come up with." Mr. Collins took a long swig of his coffee. "This is an excellent roast." Mrs. Collins patted him on the shoulder.

"There's a few blokes I served with who run a private security firm," David said. "I've spoken with them, and they can have a team assembled to protect Amanda in the next twenty-four hours if we wish."

"Nope. I don't make enough to cover private security, and Mom and Dad are close to retirement. We aren't going to break the bank for it," Amanda said, pushing her plate aside and shaking her head.

"I'm afraid this is non-negotiable, Collins." Eddie jumped to his feet. "I'll pay for whatever it costs. Money is not an issue."

Why can't she see how important this is? Clara went through this and now it's her turn! I will not leave her unprotected!

Amanda immediately objected, her eyes narrowing. "Absolutely not, Eddie. You can't throw money at the problem. Won't you anger the taxpayers? I thought that was a significant concern with your trust becoming a self-sustaining enterprise. Besides, your dad has it right. I'm still a private citizen."

"There is no price on safety," Mrs. Collins said. "Eddie, we can't allow you to bankroll the security. Tom and I will pay for whatever it costs. We have some investments we can roll over and—"

Eddie interrupted her. "What if I offered to marry you, Amanda? Would you accept the reformed Prince of Wales? I love you, and we would eventually marry anyway. That way you will be a member of my family and entitled to protection." He got down onto one knee. Adrenaline rushed through his body, his hands shaking with adrenaline.

Everyone spoke at once. The kitchen erupted into chaos. Amanda's answer was the only one Eddie cared about.

Her eyes widened in shock. All the blood drained from her face. "No. What are you thinking? Now you're just reacting to the situation. You can't just throw everything together. It doesn't work that way. More importantly, you love me?"

Eddie stood, dejected by her immediate refusal to his impulsive proposal. Mr. Collins appeared unamused, glaring. Mrs. Collins smiled and held her hands together, watching the couple carefully. Clara face-palmed.

David clapped his hands together to get everyone's attention. "Listen here!" Everyone stopped and turned to him. "That's better. I should've mentioned this up front, but the chaps are doing this as a favor to me. Voluntarily. Free. At no charge."

"Oh," Amanda managed to get out.

Eddie looked downcast at the floor. *I picked a horrible time to tell her I love her. I thought the proposal wasn't that bad of an idea.*

Mr. Collins appeared in a much better mood after David's announcement.

Clara went to stand next to her fiancé with a sigh. "And you give me a hard time for not getting the entire story out. As David mentioned, we just need to provide transportation, food, and shelter for the team. That won't be a problem. Amanda is staying with us until she is cleared to travel, and we have a better idea of just what exactly the future holds."

Amanda's face had regained some color. "I think I need to speak to Eddie alone about what he just said, outside," she stuttered.

"I think that would be a brilliant idea." He followed her toward the door and opened it for her.

Chapter Thirty

AMANDA

The morning rain had finally stopped. It was a balmy October morning as Eddie took a seat next to Amanda on David and Clara's newly acquired porch swing. There was only one person she wanted to hear from right now.

She exhaled. "I'm going to ask you some serious questions in a moment, but first, can we talk about how much I need to look into getting my own porch swing when I'm back in LA? Not that I can put it outside, but maybe in my living room. I don't need a couch."

"You always start off with whatever pops into your mind. I know you're upset at me, but at least you're still you. Never change that, Collins." Eddie jumped up, stuck his hands into his pockets, and looked out onto the palace grounds. "We have always been brutally honest with one another. I thought marriage would be the solution to all of our problems. It keeps you near me and guarantees your safety."

Amanda's eyes widened. *Eddie is so worked up. It's the stress of his training and of his depth of caring. He really did think this was the best solution to our problems.*

"Eddie…" Her voice softened, and she patted the spot next to her. "Sit." She felt her heart pick up its pace a few beats.

"We went from friends to becoming a dating couple pretty quickly. I'm crazy about you. I always have been," Amanda said, taking a breath. "I care about you way more than any other guy I've been with before. You are my first serious boyfriend. When you said you loved me in the kitchen, do you realize that was the first time I've heard it from you? That's why we needed to talk. I needed to tell you in person I love you too. I joked about it in the hospital when I sent you off to shower and shave, but I want you to know, from the bottom of my heart, I love you."

Eddie took a seat in the indicated spot. "I've loved you for a long time, Collins. I should have told you that so many times. I was too scared to do so at the hospital. I'm so afraid of mucking this relationship up. You're the first woman I've loved to the point my heart will burst if I lose you. I'm afraid I can't be the man you expect me to be. I am not a normal person. I'm a royal. My world and job were decided for me the moment I was born," Eddie said, his voice hoarse.

Amanda leaned in closer to him. "We still have so many lessons to learn about one another. I need time to process the depth of the emotions I feel about you. I don't want you to feel rushed or pressured into anything. While I embrace being your girlfriend wholeheartedly, I don't think either one of us is yet ready to be engaged. I'll get there, but I'm not ready."

Amanda reflected back on their last few months together. She hesitated. "You caught me off guard. I need to know you've thought everything through about being with me. I want us to have been together for at least a year. To have experienced a major fight, to know that there is no better life partner for us out there. I love you and want you to be absolutely certain I am the one for you. I don't want you to just decide to marry me just because."

He licked his lips. "Amanda, you are my world. You are my one and only. There will never be another woman for me. You make me feel complete. My heart is yours. I'll be waiting for you forever and always, no matter what, even if I have to wait an eternity for you." His voice was breathless.

Moving toward Eddie, Amanda closed her eyes and let his tender lips meet hers. Fireworks erupted in her head. She leaned into him as much as her body could tolerate. He tenderly left a trail of kisses on her hand, leading all the way up her cast to her neck.

"Let me show you how much I worship you," Eddie whispered into her ear.

Amanda's body felt hot. She shivered with pleasure as she detected his passion. Then the rain returned and small droplets interrupted them. She groaned. Of all the times for it to rain, it just had to be now.

"Eddie, we have to go inside. I can't risk getting sick or getting the cast wet."

His plump lips stopped nuzzling her neck, and he and Amanda slowly walked back inside, his hands interlocked with her good arm. She wasn't the only one whose body felt hot.

Eddie and Amanda returned to the apartment, their faces flushed. Her father didn't seem too aware of how flustered they appeared. Clara threw a dish towel over Amanda's neck, hiding the evidence of what had taken place outside. Eddie and Amanda coyly snuck looks at one another. Her mother chuckled at the sight of her daughter.

Amanda was positive she saw between the lines.

Her mom helped pack away the leftovers from breakfast.

"I see you've both worked out your differences. Excellent. From the way you two have been dancing around one another, it's about time. Tom and David have worked out most of the security details. I'll leave David to explain the lot."

He took over. "Right, then. We've decided that it would be most appropriate to always have a minimum of two security team members with you whenever you step out of the palace complex."

Eddie raised an eyebrow at his cousin.

"So, you've decided without input from either Eddie or me," Amanda challenged.

Her father matched her stare. "Yes, Amanda. There is no room for maneuverability."

"Okay. It was worth a shot. If that's what it takes to be with my man, then I'm cool with it. It's a small price to pay." She didn't see a point in opposing the security matter.

I won't be leaving the grounds for a while anyway.

Eddie nodded. "Thank you for coming up with a viable solution. I'll have Jonathan and my team coordinate with the Leeds team and now Amanda's team."

David and Clara nodded to one another, hands intertwined. "Seeing as everyone is here, except Princess Charlotte, David and I have some news to share with you all." Clara cleared her throat as the occupants of the room moved toward the edge of their seats. She glowed with an inner radiance, the excitement evident in her demeanor.

"You've decided on the dog you're getting?" Amanda jumped in.

Clara shook her head. "No. Even better. We can officially announce to you that we have set a date for the wedding. We've always had a chosen week, but never a specific date until now. Princess Charlotte has taken on planning most of the wedding details, but David and I thought April twenty-ninth would be the best fit for everyone. We want to be ahead of the ceremonial season, so you'll have fewer engagements to worry about, Eddie."

Amanda nearly jumped out of her seat. She gripped the table in front of her, her hands turning white.

I have to remember not to do that again. Ribs.

She took a moment to compose herself. "I am soooooooooooooo excited for you two. My bestie is officially getting married!"

Eddie clapped his hands in delight. "All right, mate. About time. It's only a few months from now. Mother and Father will be overjoyed."

"We want you to both know we expect you to be the best man and maid of honor." Clara said.

"YES!" Eddie and Amanda shouted at the same time. He clapped David on the back.

"You didn't even have to ask!" Amanda offered her good arm to the happy couple. Then she started singing in key and snapping. "Is anyone else picking up good vibrations?" Everybody eyed her and laughed. Not a single one of them joined in.

Guess I'm done with Beach Boys music for now. The Beatles may be a winner in this household, but that can't stop this California girl from trying.

Eddie shook his head and rubbed his chin. "You know, I'm surprised Auntie Charlotte hasn't been gabbing about the big date yet. She's had several binders put together for you and Clara since you told her about the engagement."

David dropped Clara's hand and fidgeted with his tie as he spoke. "I'll tell my mum next week. Clara and I would like a little more time before she reaches a whole level of excitement that we're not quite ready to cope with." Clara patted David's hand.

Amanda silently studied David. He appeared slightly more relaxed, but still she felt the urge to call him out to be less of a workaholic.

He wasn't this bad when we first met. I have to find a way to help him out. Adding wedding stress to the equation is going to push him over the edge.

"Mr. and Mrs. Collins, we want you to be involved too. As you know, I consider you to be my second parents," Clara said, her eyes misting over. "I was hoping you might stand in for as the mother and father of the bride." Amanda's mom gleefully rushed over to Clara and hugged her as she would her own daughter.

"Oh, honey, of course! We would do anything for you," she said into Clara's ear.

"Mr. Collins, can I also ask you to give me away on the big day?" Clara peeked up from behind Amanda's mother.

Her father wiped a stray tear from his face. "Absolutely. I'd be upset if you hadn't asked me. And it's Tom and Imogen, as we have asked you to call us many times." He stood as Clara was released by a joyful Mama Collins and kissed Clara on the forehead.

Chapter Thirty-One

EDDIE

The touching scene wasn't lost on Eddie. He now understood this was how he wanted the plans for his own wedding to unfold when the time came. He and Amanda needed their family and friends around them to provide the love and support for taking the next step in the rest of their lives.

The time will come, Amanda Tabitha Collins. You're the woman I want to make my Princess of Wales. Just you wait. When the time is right, I'll propose to you.

April 29 was going to come up quickly. He had quite a few logistics to figure out on his end. Eddie wondered if that would be the right time to propose properly to Amanda. He needed to let events unfold on their own, although it wouldn't hurt to initiate a few conversations with Mr. Collins and his father.

Eddie knew what his end goal was, but how could he get to that point? Clara and David's wedding would be the perfect outlet of distraction. Would it be too soon? The rejection he felt earlier couldn't feel much worse.

"Clara, how could you hold this from me for so long? I've

been hounding you about a date for weeks!" Amanda's excitement was contagious. Eddie felt himself feeding off her energy.

"We literally just decided in the early hours of this morning, A. You are the first set of people we've said anything to. Even the king has yet to be informed. David is meeting with him tomorrow." Clara relaxed as David broke out the champagne.

"It's still morning, you know," Mr. Collins joked to David.

"A little drink won't hurt." He shook his head and poured Mr. Collins the smallest possible amount.

Eddie refused the drink altogether. "None for me."

David shot him a questioning look.

"The lads and I made a pact that none of us would have a drink until everyone is through to Knightsbridge and graduates to official duty." Eddie felt somewhat uncomfortable at forgoing the celebration, but he intended to keep his promise.

"I respect that, son." Mr. Collins eyed him with a glimmer of approval. Eddie puffed out his chest, appreciating the acknowledgment.

"Well, here is to the happy couple. To the Duke and Duchess of Leeds!" The occupants of the room toasted David and Clara.

Mr. and Mrs. Collins departed London for Seattle in the early evening after a short delay. Mrs. Collins's suitcases were significantly over the weight limit. It took the combined efforts of Amanda and her father to pack everything just so.

Chapter Thirty-Two

EDDIE

Eddie cherished his moments with Amanda and his family beyond all others, relying on them during the toughest of times. Transitioning back into the life of a cavalry soldier—mucking out stables, polishing horse tack, and the constant falling off his horse—was a rude awakening after three days off.

The twelve men in Eddie's training course were now more than halfway through tier training. They were expected to all walk, trot, canter, and attempt some beginner jumps with their horses. Even for a seasoned rider like Eddie, jumping in an army-issued saddle continued to be exceedingly difficult. He still fell off his horse a handful of times.

Eddie took it in stride. The Ride—as the group of twelve was called—was close to nearing their departure from Windsor for London. In six weeks, everything would culminate with their formal graduation. Everything they learned would be on display to their loved ones and a select few members of the public. Nobody wanted to fail in front of such an audience; they had all had put extra effort into honing their skills.

Time flew by. All too soon, the Ride progressed through weeks eleven and twelve. The energy of the group intensified when they reached London, where everything became more real. Some of the blokes in the group had never before ventured to the capital city.

The sheer number of people overwhelmed the country boys. They marveled over the buildings and tourist sites their bus drove past. For Eddie, leaving the familiar barracks at Windsor brought him one step closer to Amanda, who was still recovering at Kensington Palace.

"We have some news for you, lads. You'll be taking part in your first ceremonial duties with the upcoming visit of the president of France," Corporal Reed announced at the end of their second riding session of the day.

The troopers exchanged murmurs and glances. "You will not be riding in the escort of the king; however, you will be experiencing what it is like to wear a full state kit and be expected to march up and down stairs and draw your swords appropriately when asked."

The recruits snickered.

"You boys think marching up stairs is an easy task, do you?" Corporal Reed was not amused. His mouth flattened into a tight line.

Everyone quickly closed their mouths. The riding ring grew dead silent.

"No, sir!" they exclaimed.

"Meet me on the drill square as soon as your tack and horses are stabled," the corporal yelled. "Now get to it!"

"Yes, sir," they answered, dismounting from their horses and running to put their gear away.

"Trooper Wales, are you lollygagging? Hurry it along!" Eddie sprinted to join the others.

Chapter Thirty-Three

AMANDA

Amanda was feeling a lot better as the next few weeks flew by. Her concussion symptoms had finally begun to wane. While she enjoyed puzzles, gardening, and scrapbooking, she was more than ready to begin reading, watching TV, and using her phone and computer again.

Dr. Evans was instrumental in getting Amanda back on her feet. Her hard cast was off, and she was now in a sling, ready for physical therapy. Her shoulder was extraordinarily stiff. It was a slow and arduous process that required keeping the joint loose, rebuilding movement in the elbow, wrist, and hand, and not overtaxing her weakened muscles. She needed to keep the joints mobile to avoid developing arthritis.

Amanda was at a crossroads. Her savings account was running scarily low after paying for an unused apartment and her monthly bills. The responsible side of her didn't want to mention a word of her situation to her parents or to Eddie, but the realistic half of her knew she needed to find an answer to her financial troubles soon.

While she was officially cleared for travel, she still couldn't lift anything. Finding a job that didn't require using her weakened arm would be challenging. On top of that, she dearly loved the time she was spending in the UK with David, Clara, and Eddie when he was able to chat via video with her.

Eddie was off on his own adventure, committed to army life for the next few years. Where did that put her?

Where do I see myself? Where do I fit in? Am I ready to go home? Do I want to?

She was due to meet with Pacific Skyways to discuss her recovery progress any day now. She would have a better idea of what was to come then. Something in the back of Amanda's mind felt off, but she couldn't quite put her finger on it. If she had asked herself the same questions prior to the car accident, the answer would have been a resounding "return to LA."

Have I changed because of Eddie? I've been living in my own world for almost three weeks. Having security isn't as terrible as I thought it would be. My movements aren't too restricted.

The press had died down over the last week. The strongly worded joint statements issued by Buckingham Palace on behalf of David, Eddie, and the king called out the press for assaulting her at the hospital. It had gone a long way in turning the public Amanda's way. Her English roots also assisted.

For now, Amanda, kept her adventures around London on the down-low.

I don't miss SoCal like I thought I would. My world has become based in London. I don't want to go back to LA. This is home.

The more she considered her options and reflected on her future, the more she wanted to be in London. Growing up, Amanda's dream was to become a flight attendant the moment she was age-eligible, yet she had started on the college path in order to appease her parents; it hadn't been for her.

The idea of being a flight attendant stemmed from her

grandmother Collins. Flying in the 1950s and 1960s was, by many, considered to be the golden age of aviation. In modern times, with everything being so accessible, the world was a very different place.

When I was eighteen, my dream was to travel the world. I've done that and I've had some pretty crazy adventures. However, I'm changing. Travel doesn't hold the same priority for me as being with Eddie. Am I ready to give it all up?

Before any conversations with Eddie, Amanda needed to feel out her options and how her transfer request was coming along. Summoning her courage when she was sure she was alone in her suite, she placed a call to Pacific Skyways Flight Operations in Seattle.

The automated voice answered her call. "Thank you for calling the Pacific Skyways Flight Operations Headquarters. If you are an employee seeking assistance in English, please enter your employee ID number followed by the pound key."

Amanda entered the required information and waited. In the background, she played "Fun, Fun, Fun" from Clara's laptop and tidied up some of David's scattered papers while on hold.

Navigating the phone tree to connect with a person proved to be far more challenging than she anticipated. As she waited, Amanda meticulously organized the invoices, meeting notes, general emails, and scheduling information that David left scattered about throughout the first floor. Like Eddie, he seemed to print everything.

Is this what the passengers have to deal with when they call? This definitely needs to be streamlined. If I were corporate, I'd set up a direct number. It would be sooooooo much easier. For a multimillion-dollar company, it's sad they're so slow.

A good thirty minutes later, Amanda finally reached a live person! She put down the stack of project proposals for Waleeds.

"Hello, Ms. Collins. Thanks for reaching out to the flight attendant human resources team. I've got your case number in front of me. My name is Justine. How may I be of assistance to you today?"

Ha! Even my caseworker sounds like she's speaking with a passenger. She doesn't need to be so formal.

"Hi, Justine. I'm just calling to follow up on my case. I was told to reach out to the airline when I received the medical green light to travel. I've forwarded two sets of doctor's notes to HR, just as directed. They've mentioned I need shoulder surgery for some ligament damage," Amanda explained, her nerves tingling.

"Thanks for sending these over, Amanda. I'm just looking through them now. Please hold on for a few moments." Justine clicked away and placed her on a brief hold. More elevator music played in the background. She sighed.

After about ten minutes, the caseworker returned to the line. "To clarify, the surgery is necessary for you to resume full duty, correct?"

"Yes. That's right." Amanda sucked in her breath. She didn't like Justine's tone of voice.

"I need to inform you that until further notice, you've been placed on leave," the caseworker relayed, confirming her expectations. "Additionally, based on the information I have, considering you'll be out for at least six months and unfit for your regular job duties, I am recommending your release from the company."

Amanda frowned, struggling to process this. "Hold on. Let me get this straight. You want to terminate me because I was in a car accident?" Her instincts told her something wasn't right. "I've been a member of the company for more than five years. Doesn't that count for anything? Are there any options, like becoming a flight attendant academy instructor?" Amanda didn't hold out much hope.

"I'd be happy to forward your record to the academy hiring team. I just need a little additional information from you. It looks like we're missing some information about your undergraduate degree."

Amanda squirmed and deflated. "I don't have a college degree. It wasn't required when I was hired."

"Oh, I see," Justine said, false sympathy in her voice. "Unfortunately, a college degree is the new requirement for all incoming flight attendants. If you decide to recertify as a flight attendant, you would be subject to this new regulation. All flight attendant academy instructors are also required to have a degree."

Amanda clenched her fists as the caseworker continued. "There have been many tough decisions that Pacific Skyways has had to make in the midst of its restructuring. I'm sorry to have to give you the news, but you may have been let go in the not-too-distant future anyway. Is there anything else you would like me to assist you with today?"

So a dumb piece of paper is going to force me out of the skies.

"No. That's it," Amanda whispered.

"I'll proceed with pausing the transfer application unless you'd still like to be considered for a London-based position," the caseworker added.

What good would that do her if she wasn't even eligible?

"Actually, you know what, never mind. I'd like to put in my two weeks' notice," Amanda admitted, going against her own rules about making emotional decisions in the heat of the moment.

This must have been how Clara felt when she told the Los Angeles Ballet Theater she was quitting.

"I'm sorry to hear that. If you require any additional assistance, feel free to reach out. I'll take care of the paperwork on our end," Justine said.

Amanda tuned out the rest of the meaningless words from

the caseworker. Anger surged within her. She tossed her phone onto the nearby cushion and sank to the floor.

I feel like I'm a fly, and I've been stepped on by a boot and thrown into a trash can.

Five years of unwavering commitment, and that was the best they could do. Irene had been right. Somehow knowing ahead of time about the upcoming changes softened the blow. But she was still seething with frustration.

Not even a "we can wait for your arm to heal." Wait until Daddy hears about this. He'll be just as upset as me. He's the only person right now who can understand how angry I am.

With a trembling hand, she dialed the familiar home number. It rang a few times, then her father answered. Amanda's body shook with a mixture of emotions. Her lips quivered, and she buried her head on her knees, letting out a few dry sobs the moment she heard that familiar voice on the other end of the line.

"Daddy. I need you," she mumbled into the phone.

Amidst her sniffles, she explained her predicament to her father. He listened patiently, concealing his thoughts until she regained some clarity. This was something she valued in him, one of the many traits he had acquired during his military service before transitioning to a career as a commercial pilot.

Feeling the need to expel her pent-up negative energy, Amanda paced the room. Her dad didn't mince words. "Honey, the airline industry is ruthless. I hate to break it to you, but you won't be the first or last person cast aside. You should know that, based on what we've both experienced with passenger service."

There was a pause before he continued. "I need to ask you objectively: How is your arm healing? Can you meet the job's standards? When I turn sixty-five, I'll be facing mandatory flying retirement myself and there isn't a darn thing I can do about it. How will you respond to this? Will you let it defeat you? As a Collins, how are you going to turn this situation in your favor?"

Amanda felt marginally better. She headed to the kitchenette, poured herself a glass of water, and drank it, her hands still trembling.

What am I learning about and taking away from all this?

"Dad, I appreciate you pointing things out to me. I think I needed a reality check."

"That's what I'm here for. Let me add a little more food for thought: Would you still be working as a flight attendant if you and Edmund became engaged in the future? Your relationship is much more serious than mine was with your mother at this stage. It's clear that that's the direction you two are headed. Even now, I worry about your safety."

In her mind's eye, she could picture her dad sitting in his home office, looking out into the green forests at her family home just outside Seattle.

"I know you and Mom were disappointed I never finished college. You weren't keen on me pursuing a career in aviation, but I truly believe it's taught me invaluable life lessons," Amanda admitted, bracing herself to confront her past choices.

"Yes, we were disappointed," her dad said quietly, "but it's only because we knew how bright you are. We wanted what we thought was best for you. You've grown into a strong and determined woman, Amanda, and we could not be prouder. Seize the opportunity. Your mother and I will both support your choices. Your future holds even greater and more promising prospects."

Amanda realized she needed to discuss this further with David and Eddie. She chatted a little longer with her dad, and then set out to find something to fill her time until David returned home. Stress baking seemed like a good idea.

Chapter Thirty-Four

AMANDA

Amanda vigorously mixed the flour into her mixing bowl, creating a flurry of white powder in the air. She blew a few stray hairs out of her face. Spice bottles, fresh fruit cuttings, and various other ingredients littered the counters of David and Clara's kitchen.

Using her non-dominant hand to indulge in her baking whim was a challenging experience. She hoped Clara and David might be able to assist with the cleanup later on, enticed by the promise of freshly baked scones and cookies.

In a distracted manner, she started making a list of tasks that would need to be taken care of before Clara's big day. She had selected Eddie's sister Princess Alice, Dr. Evans's daughter Jenna Evans, and their old roommate from Seattle, Olive Nakamura, as her other bridesmaids. Amanda chuckled at the thought of a princess, a ballet student, and an ex-Olympic gymnast coming together—what a unique blend of personalities.

We haven't spoken to Olive for who knows how long. She's gonna be shocked when she hears I'm leaving aviation! I wonder when Clara might want to start looking at bridal gowns and bridesmaid dresses. Princess Charlotte said something about lilac, white, and silver for a color scheme. Clara hasn't mentioned a dress yet. She better get on it.

Amanda didn't have to wait too long for David's return, as he arrived earlier than expected to change clothes before his weekly dinner with his mother. She moved from the kitchen to the formal dining room. With Clara still at rehearsal, David had taken advantage of the empty table and carefully spread out seven or eight different piles of papers to examine.

Over the course of several months, David's work habits had undergone a regression to his pre-Clara routines. The shift occurred just as the Waleeds Trust portfolio and his shoe company, Leeds of London, experienced exponential growth. If there was a man who needed an assistant, it was David.

"Leeds-man! How's it going? I was hoping I could catch you. I wanted to get your opinion on something," Amanda chimed in with a playful tone.

She and David shared an ongoing joke. The more time she spent in his home and the more they got used to each other, the more at ease she felt. Their friendship was evolving, reaching a point where David felt like family.

He was Clara's "leeding" man, a pun on his royal title and Clara's profession. He seemed to embrace it wholeheartedly. Amanda had envisioned the conversation about handing in her notice and searching for a new position, but it didn't quite unfold the way she had anticipated.

"AC! I thought the room felt cooler in here." David grinned.

His eyes seemed tired, displaying faint purple circles that hinted at sleepless nights. It was a bit challenging to discern behind his glasses, something Amanda found concerning. She decided to switch her approach.

"You look lousy. What's on your mind?" she asked.

She prepared a fresh cup of coffee for both of them and

continued working on finishing her scones. The initial batch of cookies had given her a sense of confidence in her ability to bake with just one hand.

David removed his glasses and pinched the bridge of his nose. "Seems like nothing ever slips by you, huh?"

Amanda shrugged with her left arm. "Call it the hidden talent of a flight attendant. Seriously, spill the beans. What's going on?"

David watched as she puttered around his kitchen. She tapped the wooden stirring spoon on the side of her mixing bowl.

This is the best workout for my arm to get back up to strength. Building up the wrist and elbow.

Gratefully accepting the steaming coffee mug Amanda offered, David opened up. "I've overstretched myself and now I don't know what to do. Between my mother, the wedding, and all the Waleeds stuff, there aren't enough hours in the day. It's one meeting after another, and then I feel guilty for neglecting Clara and not being there enough for her."

Amanda set her bowl aside and sat down next to him at the dining table, attentively nodding as David shared his concerns. She shuffled a few of his papers carefully out of harm's way, mindful not to disturb anything. She wiped her hands on her apron.

David needed a person to confide in, especially without Eddie around. He rarely let his guard down with anyone, except possibly Clara.

I am the lucky person to crack the Duke of Leeds. If only David had a way to add more hours to the day, or a time machine. I need to find Marty McFly or Doc Brown.

"This coffee is wonderful. Just the shot of caffeine I needed. But let's shift the focus back to you. What did you want to discuss?" David inquired.

Amanda steered him back to the topic at hand. "My

problem can wait a moment. Have you talked to Clara about how you're feeling, or your mom? And what about Eddie?"

"No. Mother is the wedding planner. Clara is focusing on her run of a million and one Swan Lakes and Nutcrackers coming up. She needs all the rest she can get, without the added stress," David explained, making valid points.

The Nutcracker always took a toll on Clara every holiday season. She was at the theater four to five times a week, in addition to her regular rehearsals. Amanda shuddered, thinking back to her endless runs to the store for Epsom salt for her bestie to soak her feet in. Clara's feet suffered every winter.

"I understand. Eddie has enough on his plate—he's essentially married to the army. You need a robot, or a TARDIS telephone box," Amanda suggested, making a reference to *Doctor Who*.

"Indeed, I'd love to have a TARDIS around. However, until it materializes, I'm a one-man operation. What I really need to do is hire someone to help with Waleeds. It's grown faster than I anticipated. My private secretary handles my royal engagements and has helped with getting Leeds of London off the ground, but I can't ask him to help with Waleeds too."

David paused for another sip of his coffee. The oven timer went off. Amanda stood, headed over, and opened the door to check on the cookies' progress. The delightful aroma of chocolate filled the room. "Mind helping me take these out?"

She handed David a pair of oven mitts, gesturing toward the cooling rack as the tray of soft, doughy cookies emerged to cool.

Meanwhile, Amanda hunted for a spatula. "Have you considered using Waleeds as a segue into your shoe company? What if you were to put out a call for people who might be keen on learning how to make shoes and offered them an apprenticeship through the Waleeds Trust at Leeds of London?"

She continued talking as she stirred the scone mix and poured it onto two empty sheets on the kitchen island. "Once they complete their apprenticeship, you could bring them on as shoemakers, giving them a valuable trade and guaranteed employment. They could become the teachers to the next group." Amanda's thoughts raced. "You're the one who told me shoe making is a dying art."

David turned his gaze to her, and the lines on his face softened into a handsome smile. "That's a brilliant suggestion. Now I just have to find a way to make it happen."

She felt flattered to hear his excitement. The disappointment from earlier in the day was replaced by contentment. It was gratifying to lend a hand with someone else's problems. She offered him a forced smile.

"Amanda, what's going on?" David inquired, concern furrowing his brow. "It's written all over your face. Your smile normally reaches your eyes. You look like I do—stressed."

She grimaced and stared at the misshapen lobes of her scones. Some were oval, some circular, some appeared more like blobs. She adjusted the temperature on the oven and made the motions to place the trays in. David quietly stepped in, still wearing the oven mitts. She set the kitchen timer for twenty minutes.

Letting out a sigh, Amanda returned to the cooling racks and scooped up a few cookies, avoiding eye contact with David. "Before you came home, I called Pacific Skyways. The news wasn't encouraging. The truth is, I think I decided a while ago that aviation doesn't make my heart sing anymore. Eddie does. I gave the airline my notice."

Tears welled up in Amanda's eyes, her shoulders slumping in defeat. She dropped the spatula. "I don't know where to go from here."

David moved to stand beside her and offered her a tissue. She dabbed at her eyes, and he hugged her, mindful of her still tender and healing arm. After a moment, he released her.

"This is a conversation you need to have with Eddie. From personal experience, major life-altering decisions are a two-person job. I know you. You'll figure something out. For what it's worth, I can't imagine you in just any job. It needs to align with your personality. Outside of aviation, what are you passionate about?"

Amanda wiped her eyes dry, considering her options. "The creative side of me loves shopping, outdoor activities like hiking, and cooking." She hesitated, then added, "But the intellectual side of me likes to solve problems. I really like Sudoku and math-related things. At one point in time, I was a math major."

"That doesn't at all surprise me," David exclaimed, his smile radiant. "The answer you're looking for will come to you when you least expect it. Speaking to Eddie should definitely help. Don't delay too long."

Amanda leaned against the kitchen island, feeling more upbeat. David's eyes lingered longingly on the cookies she had made. She nodded, indicating he could enjoy them. He grabbed a plate from the cabinet and placed two cookies onto it.

He winked playfully. "It might be a good idea if you were to hide the tray from me, otherwise I may eat the lot. You're even more talented than the chefs employed by the palace. Clara and I should hire you to create our wedding menu."

Amanda froze. *Why didn't I think of this earlier?*

"Feel free to say no to this, but would you be open to hiring me as a part-time assistant for the Waleeds Trust? I'm already pretty familiar with what your and Eddie's visions for the foundation are, and it would give me something meaningful to do," she said, glancing at the kitchen timer. The scones still had a few more minutes in the oven.

David smiled. "I don't even need to think about it. Of course you're hired. You can set your own pay and hours and let me know what you're comfortable assisting me with. I don't want to overwhelm you."

He reached for another cookie.

Amanda gently slapped his hand. "No more cookies." They laughed, and she continued, "Awesome! I'm totally happy to start today. I've been itching to reorganize the loads of papers you've been bringing home. I've already tried to sort some of it for you when I tidy up."

David rubbed his chin. "I was wondering why the briefs and other reports were arranged differently. You've been doing a bang-up job."

Amanda smiled brightly. "I have dual citizenship, so it shouldn't be too difficult to formalize any employment paper-work. Do you have time to answer a couple questions for me?"

"For you, absolutely."

Chapter Thirty-Five

EDDIE

Eddie's group breathed a collective sigh of relief. The most challenging part of the inspection was over for now. The officer in charge had scrutinized them thoroughly. He seemed to know exactly where to find fault with each recruit, especially the new pieces of their kit they were not yet accustomed to wearing or cleaning.

How were they to know the heavy metal cuirasses breast-plates they were wearing weren't shiny enough? Or that the excess wax on their boots would be an issue? The Ride was looking at a few more hours of polishing once the Corporal of Horse was satisfied with their drill.

Marching up and down stairs in their thigh-high jackboots was more challenging than it seemed. The boots severely restricted their freedom of movement. What's more, once they were polished, the recruits had to adapt walking with a waddle to avoid creasing the polish on the boots. Eddie chuckled at the thought of Amanda watching him.

"Mate, are you going to give us a full tour of the palace after we're off parade today?" Vince joked as they headed back to the changing room to carefully stow their helmets, swords, and other ceremonial kit items away.

Eddie leaned against his locker. "That depends on what's in it for me. You always finish your polishing quickly. If you take my sword to the armory for sharpening, I'll consider it. Maybe you'd fancy a tour of my room. I've got a top-of-the-line big-screen telly and gaming system."

Vince frowned. "Nah, I have my own gaming rig at my parents' flat. What about the rooms the public don't usually have access to?"

"I've always wondered meself what you lot live like," another soldier, Jack, added.

The group's attention turned to Eddie. "Tell you what. We are due for a big celebration after the graduation pass-out ride. What if the festivities were celebrated at the palace? You chaps can choose between either Kensington Palace or Buckingham Palace. I don't really care to see Windsor again anytime soon."

I can't see why my parents would object. Added bonuses of seeing Amanda and the blokes thinking I'm a hero for the VIP access.

The recruits chatted amongst themselves. "I guess that will have to do," one of them said.

"You blokes can invite your families. I'm sure my parents would love to meet them. Maybe don't tell them until the day of the event. People tend to get a bit uptight and anxious when they're presented to my father. He's just another military man. Nothing too special," Eddie said, trying to downplay the situation.

"Blimey. Having our families meet the king? Me mum would be indebted to me forever." Jack grinned at the thought.

"Fantastic. It's settled, then." Eddie closed his locker. "I'll have my girl relay the message to my cousin."

"Make sure you thank her for the care package too. Any chance she can include some biscuits with the next one?" Vince asked.

~

"Eddie! Can you please look at me when we chat? I promise I won't keep you long," Amanda's frustrated voice called out.

Eddie glanced up from his desk at the image of Amanda reclining on a sofa. He placed his polishing rag down and closed his container of boot polish. "Sorry, I have a lot to do." He ran his hand through his hair. His fingers itched to continue with his polishing.

"I wanted you to know how excited I am for you!" Amanda said with pride in her voice. "This is going to be the first television program I get to watch since the accident! Should I make popcorn? Do you want me to record it?"

Eddie leaned back in the small desk chair in the room he shared with two others.

"Collins, I won't be on telly for more than a second, if at all. The news tends to only show the state coach and foot soldiers marching up the Royal Mall. It's not even that glamorous. It's not worth making a big deal over."

Eddie turned to his laughing roommates. "Can you two shut it? I'm trying to chat with my girlfriend." They shot him a glare and stepped out of the room.

"I finally have the room to myself. I have no idea why Ian and Jack were making all that noise. Now, what is it you wanted to talk about?" He balanced the phone on his desk, giving himself the freedom to use his hands.

Amanda frowned. "Was that any way to treat your roommates? Eddie, even for you, that was rude."

His eyes twitched. He had a tension headache beginning to build.

Maybe I can get five hours of sleep tonight.

Amanda bit her lip. "Look, what I have to say can wait if you have other things to do. You're obviously tired. Go find your roommates and apologize. We can talk tomorrow."

"Amanda, I'm sorry, it's been a long day. Ian and Jack are probably just as dead on their feet as I am. I'm just trying to be there for you." Eddie winced as his voice came across as harsher than he intended. He knew he needed to apologize to his roommates. He felt guilty for snapping at them.

Amanda's brow creased. "I understand you're stressed. I've been there too. I just wanted to involve you in the conversation so you wouldn't feel left out."

Eddie's shoulders sagged. She was trying to include him and give him a voice in her life. If they truly wanted their relationship to succeed, he realized he needed to put in the same amount of effort as Amanda. He rubbed his eyes, feeling the weight of the day.

"First, how would you feel about me joining the Waleeds Trust part-time?" she said, her voice softening. "I'd be handling the administrative tasks."

Eddie's voice was cautious. "Why would you want to work for us? I thought you wanted to try to transfer here to London with the airline? You love flying."

Amanda looked down from the screen, her cheeks flushed. "I just wanted to discuss the idea with you. Nothing has been decided yet. David was feeling really stressed, and I know you've been busy. I'm aware of some of the projects you and David wanted to undertake, and I just thought it would be the perfect way to help everyone out and be closer to you. I need some income while I'm recovering."

There had to be more to her story. Amanda didn't normally get flustered so easily. She wasn't the same happy-go-lucky woman he'd come to know before the accident. Why hadn't he noticed it earlier?

"Collins, be straight with me," he pleaded. "What happened?"

A few tears rolled down Amanda's cheeks. "Eddie, I handed in my resignation today. There's been some unforeseen issues with some of the soft tissue in my shoulder. I need a couple updated scans, but at this stage, it looks like there's a possibility I might need surgery."

"Surgery?"

She nodded. "I'll be out longer than expected, and that means I'd have to recertify as a flight attendant. Oh, Eddie, it's awful. They have this new requirement where all the incoming FAs have to be college grads, but I never finished college. On top of that, I've burned through my savings. I'm too proud to ask my parents for help. I feel so lost."

Eddie jumped out of his seat and held his phone closer to his face. "Hey, hey, hey. No tears. We'll figure this out. We are both running on empty. I'm sorry for being short with you earlier, Amanda. This needs to be a deeper and longer conversation. I'm fine if you want to work with Waleeds. Actually, it's a brilliant idea. I don't want you to worry about money. I understand it's a sensitive subject. Worst case, you could borrow from me and pay me back when you can. I just want you to get a good night's sleep. It's important for your health and your recovery. I want nothing more than to take you in my arms and never let you go."

Amanda wiped her face with her sleeve. "Look, I picked a bad time to discuss this. I've been keeping all this to myself, and now it's pouring out. I've been an emotional mess, I promise I'll get some shut-eye tonight, and I hope you can too. Let's talk again tomorrow. I love you."

"I promise, and I love you too." Eddie blew a kiss at the screen and clicked his phone off, closed his eyes, and fought off a yawn.

He needed to find Ian and Jack. He could be an arse when

he was cranky. But first, he wanted to make sure someone checked on Amanda. The wheels in his mind began to turn. How could he have a special night out with her? She needed a change of scenery.

He sat up straighter and dialed a familiar phone number. "Hi, Clara. It's Eddie. I need your help."

He hadn't been able to do nearly as much for Amanda as she deserved. It was time to show her how amazing she was.

Chapter Thirty-Six

EDDIE

Eddie owed the guys big time for covering for his absence. Under the guise of being called away to the palace, Eddie managed, in his very limited free time, to slip out to Kensington Palace. It was almost nine in the evening. Sneaking out of Knightsbridge could get him in a heap of trouble with his superiors, but for Amanda, it was a risk he was willing to take. Their conversation three days ago had struck a chord with him.

Clara had cleared the dance studio on the second floor of the flat she shared with David. As a special gift, David had wanted her to have the ability to practice at home whenever she needed it, or if she just needed a space to be in her creative zone, as she called it.

The room was dominated by floor-to-ceiling mirrors on three walls and had a large bay window on the fourth. Two portable ballet bars were moved to the corners of the room near Clara's yoga mat.

Despite their nightly chats, it was agony for Eddie to know Amanda was in the guest suite two floors below, and not be able to see her in person.

"This is the space I thought would work best. Amanda never comes in here except for physical therapy, and that's only when I'm supervising. Your secret will be safe for now," Clara offered. "Go ahead and warm up."

Eddie's eyes widened. *Warm up? What does she expect? Should I do what I normally do at the gym?*

She took pity on him and explained he needed to limber up just enough not to hurt his body. She usually did some crunches, push-ups, and other Pilates exercises. Eddie followed her example.

"I've had a couple of ballroom dance lessons Mum forced on me in the past, but never any other type of social dancing." Eddie admitted, unsure of where to begin.

He moved to the center of the room, dressed in a pair of black sweatpants, socks, and a T-shirt. Clara clicked on the familiar "Stomping at the Savoy" music from the *I Love Lucy* episode they were trying to re-create.

"Close your eyes and listen to the beat. Start tapping your foot once you figure out the timing and snap along with it. Muscle memory from your previous ballroom lessons should kick in. I rely on it every night," Clara said.

Eddie was skeptical of her methods although she was a professional dancer, but he needed to trust her if he wanted to surprise Amanda. He tried his best to follow her instructions, even though it felt so foreign to his body.

He couldn't keep his thoughts to himself. "This feels stupid," he said, opening his eyes.

Learning how to do a version of the jitterbug-slash-swing seemed like an easy idea after watching videos of it. Now he wasn't so sure.

Clara gave him a death stare. "Good. That means you're doing it right. The more awkward it feels, the better," she encouraged.

She clapped in time with the music, Eddie closed his eyes

once more, repeating the drill, and keeping in time with her clapping rhythm. After a few minutes, he picked up on the beat.

Clara smiled. "Now you're going to work on stepping side to side in time with the music, adding to the swing step and box steps we learned via video chat. We'll build from there. From all the videos I've watched of different versions of the jitterbug, the timing seems like the most crucial aspect. Remember, I'm not a ballroom expert."

"Does it work like that in ballet?" Eddie was genuinely curious.

"Absolutely! Everything in ballet has a purpose. The music tells the story and directs the dancer how to move," Clara explained, correcting his posture and tapping his shoulder, reminding him to relax.

He worked on getting the side-to-side step in time with the beat, gradually moving into a basic swing dance pattern.

My big feet move better than David's do. I can't get my hips to move like the video, though. Think about David's attempt to learn ballet. He's so stiff. Think opposite of my cousin.

"Better. Now, let's link arms. I'll guide you through the basic turn and chase step. Given your height, you might need to hunch slightly."

Their differences in height added an extra challenge to an already tricky situation. They needed a new approach. Clara had the brilliant idea of putting her pointe shoes on. When on her toes, she was about even with Eddie. They resumed their secret dancing practice.

I hope I don't step on her foot or break her. David and the Westminster Ballet would kill me.

Eddie tried to bounce on his feet and flailed his arms about, physically attempting to release tension from his body. Jumping up and down did help lighten up his doubtful mood.

"There we go." Clara took him and led him through the steps.

After a few minutes, he seemed to grasp the basic concept. He learned fast. Clara kept layering in different movements until finally, Eddie had enough steps to put together the very basics of their version of the jitterbug. She was an excellent teacher. Dancing was hard work. They took a quick break.

"Not bad, Eddie." Clara beamed and patted him on the back, offering him some water.

If I'm this tired now, I don't know if I'll be able to make it through the full three minutes of dancing. How does Clara do it? This is much harder than basic training or what I'm doing now.

"This is the first and only lesson we'll have for a while, right? I'll make a video of what you should practice, and maybe you can have one of your roommates practice with you."

Not bloody likely. Clara's suggestion was well-intentioned, but there wasn't a sodding chance he would even ask one of them.

"I have to get back before lights out. I have extra polishing to do for the guys covering for me. Thanks a bunch, C." Eddie kissed Clara on the cheek and gave her a big hug.

She blushed and hugged him back. "Just promise to send me pictures of your date night when it comes up. I'm so jealous! You've taken things to an entirely new level. Who knew you were such a romantic," she gushed.

Eddie packed up his bag, slipped his shoes on, and hurried to have David's loyal driver, Michael, drive him the ten minutes back to the barracks. In a week's time, his planning would come into play. But first, he needed to get past tomorrow's state visit.

Chapter Thirty-Seven

AMANDA

After they had stopped by three shops to pick up shoes and kid gloves, Amanda sensed that something significant was about to take place. She was delighted to be out and about, appreciating the abundance of shopping options in London compared to LA.

Venturing out in public after six weeks confined to Kensington Palace did wonders to lift her spirits. Clara had been lips-sealed about why Amanda needed the dress in the first place, but she didn't see a need to argue with her bestie when she willingly wanted to shop.

This is the first time I've ever been in London this long without going to Harrods or Selfridges. Of course, not really having an income puts a damper on the entire experience. If luck is on my side, my first paycheck should hit my bank account within the next week.

Although she initially struggled to keep up-to-date with being able to read David's meeting notes, project proposals, and other items, Amanda was finally caught up. The first item on her agenda was to digitize his paper mess. David had grudgingly come around to the benefits of being able to type in a keyword to find what he was looking for.

But Amanda didn't want to think about work now. She felt absolutely stunning in her vintage 1960s gown as she gazed at her radiant reflection in the dressing-room mirror. She marveled at the way the emerald dress dropped into a V, complementing her bustline perfectly. The skirt flared out at the knees, settling at a flattering tea length.

The gold belt the store owner had suggested accentuated the green, confirming her choice. It made her feel so posh and worthy of being by her prince's side. At least, she assumed this was all for a date of some sort. Suspicions had begun to grow after Clara had whisked her away for a hair and nail session.

Studying herself, she noticed a difference in her appearance—more relaxed, more mature. Amanda had embraced her natural curls, especially since straightening her hair wasn't possible with her arm in the condition it was. She reflected on the events of the past week—losing her job, finding a new one, and then learning she likely needed surgery on her shoulder.

She was still grappling with accepting the way her arms appeared lopsided due to the accident. The loss of muscle on the right side of her arm was evident, the area still bruised and swollen, limiting her range of motion. The cap sleeves on the dress hid most of the damage. Despite this, for the first time in weeks, Amanda's face lit up. She knew one thing was missing.

"C, would you mind reaching into my bag for the Dior lipstick? It's the perfect red to complement this emerald-green dress."

Clara went over to the dressing room and rummaged through Amanda's Aspinal of London bag, a new brand she had just discovered and a gift from her new boss.

Clara was slow to retrieve the lipstick. "It should be in the gray Longchamp pouch—it has the big CD on the top of it," Amanda said.

With the extra directions, Clara managed to find the desired item. "You speak a foreign language to me when you yell out brand names. In this case, the CD is helpful. Haha, it's the initials of David and me. No wonder I've always liked Dior."

She handed the lipstick to Amanda, who shifted off the fitting room pedestal and moved closer to the mirror. She glided the ruby-red color onto her lips and smacked them together.

I'm me again.

"Awwww, Amanda, you look so pretty!" Clara gushed, staring at her best friend. "This is the perfect dress for your date with Eddie. I hope you can break those shoes in before." Clara slapped a hand over her mouth, realizing the slip.

"So it is a date," Amanda teased her friend. She smiled reassuringly. "Don't worry, C, your secret is safe with me. I won't say anything. I had a feeling anyway."

With her curly red hair in a low chignon and her emerald necklace, she would be set to impress. "I haven't seen Eddie in person in about six weeks. Has it really been that long?"

Amanda longed to be able to finally have him wrap her in his long arms. After their small fight last week, both of them had been almost cautious in their conversations, sticking to safe topics such as running through the events of their day. Being around each other in person would hopefully clear up any lingering concerns and allow them to connect on a deeper, more intimate level.

"Let me take a picture to send to your mom. She'll love this!" Clara pulled out her phone and snapped a few shots.

"Vintage is always the way to go. Everything was just made better back then." Making her way back to the fitting room, Amanda slid the curtain shut to change.

"When did you start shopping for vintage things, A?" Clara asked from the waiting area.

"A lot of my bags and accessories are preloved or vintage. You get more bang for your buck that way, and it's better for the environment. I don't buy a ton of things new unless it's jewelry or a trendy bag. Remember my grandmother's bag I inherited?" Amanda said as she slid back into her jeans, riding boots, white silk shirt, and blue cardigan. She held the precious dress in her hands as they headed to the register.

Clara wrinkled her face, trying to remember back to their Seattle apartment. "Vaguely. Is it the black leather bag from Seattle?"

"That's the one. It's a black vintage Hermès Kelly from 1962. Grandmother Collins took such great care of her bag and really taught me about fashion. It's my most prized possession. That's when I learned about vintage. That bag is over fifty years old, C, and looks pristine."

Amanda handed the dress over and glanced around the shop one last time. *Do I need anything else from here? No. I better not even look. I'm shopping from my own closet.* Her generous coworker had kindly sent over a quarter of Amanda's belongings from California.

As soon as she paid, the dress was wrapped and packed up for the two ladies, and then they headed outside. Clara's security team waited for them and pulled the car up to head back to Kensington Palace.

"We have about an hour before I get to watch Eddie." Amanda glanced at her watch. "So, you really won't give me any info other than to wear this dress with my overcoat and comfy shoes next week?"

"No way, Jose. I've been sworn to secrecy. You have to wait until you see your prince in the flesh next week." Clara made the motion of zipping her lips tightly closed and throwing away the key. Amanda barked out in laughter.

"It feels so good to be out and about like we used to. I've

missed this." She looked out the window at their surroundings.

"I've been dying to ask, what are your plans now that you're on the road to recovery?" Clara attempted her own luck at prying for information.

Amanda let out a sigh. "I'm torn between beginning my own cookbook for Waleeds and working on school applications. I'm leaning toward pursuing my undergrad degree part-time here. I had two years under my belt when I dropped out. I just don't want it to clash with my upcoming maid of honor duties!"

Clara eyed her friend sympathetically. "I remember when you had to make the initial decision—school or flight attendant academy. How many credits do you need to finish?" she asked.

"I think I need about a year and a half's worth. If I went to school in London, I don't know how the credits would transfer. David seemed optimistic I could be done in a year, since British degrees are designed to be finished in three years. The more I think about it, the more appealing the idea of finishing what I started becomes," Amanda shared, turning to face Clara.

"I'm sure your parents would be thrilled. I bet your mom wants Oxford or Cambridge. University College in London is supposed to be excellent. Have you considered a culinary course? That's something I could see you doing too."

Amanda huffed. "Actually, Mom is dead set on the London School of Economics. Dad doesn't care so long as I finish this time. I want my cooking to remain enjoyable. I don't want it to be a career." She looked at Clara. "I've matured a lot in the past couple of months. I'm not the same person I was when I met Eddie. And you've changed too, my soon-to-be duchess. Everything evolves. It's just my turn." The two shared a look and laughed.

"Have you considered tying up your loose ends in SoCal.? I can't believe it's been five years. When does your lease end?" Clara asked.

"It's month to month, so whenever I decide. I still have a lot of things to sort through. I've been keeping my apartment just in case."

After talking with Clara, she felt a sense of relief. Clara had moved full-time to London just over nine months ago. Had it really been that long? Amanda had been in London for almost two months. She knew she had to remain patient for the time being. Patience was a virtue. For a fast-paced person like her, it was the world's most difficult thing to manage.

Chapter Thirty-Eight

EDDIE

Eddie and the eleven others in his ride laughed as they boarded a white transit van to get from the Knightsbridge Barracks to Buckingham Palace. They passed the one hundred and thirty mounted men and horses lined up in an impressive succession waiting to proceed out on parade.

"Make way for the royal white van. We have a VIP onboard," Victor joked.

"If they knew you were onboard, Wales, I'd wager they'd give you a pass from polishing kit," said Garret, one of the youngest recruits, from Australia.

"Not bloody likely. Let's be real, I'd be asked to hold myself well above the required standard. Wait until you lads meet my father. He is even stricter than Major Bird." Eddie laughed.

A few eyes went large. "Truly?" Vince asked.

He nodded in confirmation.

The recruits were dressed for the first time in the full uniform of the Household Cavalry, six in red tunics and six in blue tunics. The only major distinction between the two units that formed the regiment was the color of the plume on their helmets and where the strap of the helmets was placed on the soldier. Life Guards wore their chain chin straps just below the lower lip. The Blues and Royals wore theirs below the chin.

Ask any soldier, and it was a major point of contention. The regiments had merged in 2005, but maintained different horses and sleeping quarters. Still, in the age of modern warfare, they served together. In the field, the Household Cavalry drove iron horses, also known as tanks.

They were the light infantry division of the British Army. After two years in London, the recruits would have the option of serving for two years in the field. Eddie dearly wished he could be of use for his country outside of ceremonial duty, yet he understood the dangers, and as heir to the throne, it would never be possible.

Throughout his life, Eddie would always remember the men he served with. Their dedication, sacrifices, and stories would fuel his duty and commitment to giving back in any way he could.

Tourists often overlooked the fact that the ceremonial cavalry members and soldiers of the foot guards were active military and soldiers first. But for today, the goal was to stand to attention for half an hour, salute the king, and correctly march up and down steps.

The van halted and the door slid open. "Here we are lads. Welcome to Buckingham Palace." Eddie smirked.

One of the more experienced soldiers assisted the recruits with getting out of the van and handed them their jackboots as they hopped out, intended as a means to keep the boots pristine for a perfect presentation known as turnout. The soldiers didn't wear the boots in the van to keep from ruining the high polish job.

I've spent hours working on these. Best they don't get trashed now.

"All right there, recruits? You lot are now officially on

parade. Life Guards on the left, Blues and Royals to the right. Follow me and keep up. Keep your dressing tight and in formation," the commander ordered. Dressing was the army term for length between the soldiers.

The guards' quarters at Buckingham Palace weren't vastly different from those at Knightsbridge Barracks. They only stayed inside the palace walls during the forty-eight hours they were on duty. Otherwise, the foot guards stayed at Wellington Barracks just up the Royal Mall.

Eddie's eyes roamed the guard boxes and inner courtyard, where he and the others would be stationed. The feeling of the recruits was a mixture of excitement and nerves.

He reminisced about the handful of occasions he had accompanied his father from Parliament to Buckingham Palace in the state carriage. The carriage itself wasn't overly exciting. The interior was dated, very uncomfortable, and it often smelled musty. The thrill was seeing all of the people out and about, attempting to catch a glimpse of his father.

There had been many times Eddie had stepped out from the inner courtyard to the receiving rooms without giving the guards by the door a second glance. From now on, he resolved, he would always acknowledge the soldiers around him with eye contact.

For the guards on sentry duty, the goal was to be invisible. Eddie never envisioned himself blending in. He had to admit, he relished the feeling. The more difficult part was keeping a stony-faced expression.

The recruits had a final chance to practice their marching before the main event. The commanding officers demanded alertness, preparing the recruits for any potential schedule changes, though none occurred.

The call to stand to attention came quickly. "Troopers, present arms!"

The guard unit drew their swords from the scabbards and,

with perfect precision, held them upright. They were the only members of the army able to bear arms in the king's presence. At exactly 12:40 p.m., the Irish Guards' band struck up the national anthem of France, followed by "God Save the King." The moment the wheels on the golden coach stopped moving, the king made his descent from the carriage. The recruits saluted him.

Standing at attention without moving his head, Eddie schooled his face into a neutral expression and watched his father pose for a few photos with the president of France. Not a single person gave the recruits a second glance, except for one. The king's knowing eyes met his son's. Less than five minutes later, it was over.

The command to replace their swords was given. After standing still and keeping his arm locked for about thirty minutes, Eddie, like his companions, had lost feeling in his extremities. He fiddled with the sword's placement.

The soldiers lined up and marched up the steps. Eddie fell backward and missed a step, much to his displeasure. At least he wasn't the only one. Aaron, the burly, critical recruit still not on the best of terms with Eddie, fell back as well. In comparison to the beginning stages of their training, the two were at least on professional terms.

It was going so well too.

Once inside the building, the recruits received a positive acknowledgment from the commanding officer.

"Not the best marching, troopers, but considering this is your first attempt—" The officer stopped mid-sentence as the door behind him gently opened and closed.

The stunned recruits went wide-eyed and slack-jawed, momentarily forgetting their place. Entering the hallway from the receiving area was Eddie's father.

The king cleared his throat. "Gentlemen, no need to salute or kneel." Nobody moved a muscle. "I just wanted to come and introduce myself. Edmund had asked me to make myself available for the graduation parade. However, if you wouldn't mind indulging an old military man, I'd like to hear where each one of you young men is from and your name." He patiently put his arms behind his back. "We'll start with your commanding officer here."

For the first time that Eddie could recall, their commanding officer was at a loss for words. He was sorely tempted to laugh at the scene and mentally calculated the number of extra chores he would be able to pawn off on the others later this evening. Perhaps he would have time to put his plan into action tonight instead of waiting until next week.

Chapter Thirty-Nine

AMANDA

"**A**ll right, my lady, we are heading out for the evening. Save your questions about tonight until we reach our intended destination," Eddie said, offering his arm to escort Amanda to the car waiting outside apartments 1A and 1B at Kensington Palace.

I can't believe Eddie was able to sneak out tonight! As if seeing him for a split second in the press-call photos wasn't enough, I get my man in the flesh. Clara had mentioned a date for next week, not today! Eddie must have gone to a lot of trouble planning whatever we're doing tonight. This man fills my heart with joy every time I see him.

Eddie's ensemble made Amanda want to swoon. He looked stunning in a tightly tailored black tuxedo with a crisp white shirt and a black bow tie.

That tux, though… so hot! I wish I had seen more before he threw that overcoat over it. Amanda fanned herself as Eddie watched with amusement. *As if he weren't handsome enough in the cavalry uniform.*

She adjusted the garment hiding her dress. Eddie would

have to wait until they reached their intended destination to see her outfit.

"I can have the air turned on if you're overly warm," he joked.

"Nope, I'm just thinking inappropriate thoughts about you," Amanda shot back as her cheeks heated.

"The feeling is mutual. I am thinking along the same lines as you. I love it when you tell me exactly what's on your mind." Eddie grinned rakishly and leaned over to steal a kiss.

"I'm a little surprised at how snug your tux is. It looks almost too tight on you. Not that I mind one bit," Amanda said, biting her lip.

"I'll let you in on a little secret. This tux doesn't fit well. My body's changed shape since I had it made. There's a chance it may burst at the seams," Eddie confessed, blushing slightly.

"If you hulk out of it, that's fine by me." Amanda joked, impersonating the Hulk.

They both burst into laughter. "I need to control myself until after dinner, then you can properly thank me." Eddie fiddled with his bow tie.

Amanda mock saluted. "Oh! You seem confident. Okay, Mr. Big Shot. I leave everything to your capable hands."

Eddie chuckled.

If he thinks whatever he has planned for tonight is going to involve thanking him, I'm holding him to the highest possible standard. What does Princey have planned? It can't just be dancing and dinner, can it?

The black Range Rover pulled up to a private entrance of one of London's most exclusive member clubs in the Mayfair district.

"Are we having dinner here tonight?" Amanda asked, a hint of uncertainty in her voice.

Her eyes swept over the beautiful ivy-covered red-brick exterior of the Georgian-era home with two large windows. Just as the vehicle pulled up to the entrance, sparkling fairy lights turned on, providing the front of the building with a magical glimmer.

"Of course. I've rented out my members' club for the evening. Nobody here to bother us. No press, no extra security, just us and a few select members of the staff."

Eddie waited for the all-clear from his protection team. After being semi-independent in the army, Amanda surmised that it took him a while to readjust to having Jonathan and company back with him.

As Eddie stepped out of the car and waited for Amanda, she was careful not to reveal her dress yet, keeping her hands clamped over her coat to shield it from the evening breeze.

He escorted her into the building. Inside, the hallways had been decorated to make it appear as if they were entering a jungle. Exotic plants and the sound of jungle animals softly playing in the background brought out vibes from their trip to Disneyland. The receptionist bowed to Eddie.

"Your Royal Highness. We've prepared everything you've requested for yourself and your guest. Please alert the staff or me if any additional needs arise. We continue to appreciate your royal patronage here at Charlie's!" The receptionist signaled for their coats to be taken.

"Thank you." Eddie nodded to the woman and handed over his overcoat.

Amanda's own black Reiss overcoat slipped off smoothly, revealing her stunning green and gold vintage tea-length bombshell dress and matching green heels. Eddie cleared his throat. His eyes lingered on her dress longer than normal.

"I take it you approve of my ensemble." She twirled for him.

Score! He's speechless.

"I like it very much," Eddie managed, his voice cracking slightly. Amanda slid a pair of white kid gloves from her small clutch and signaled to him that the maître d' was waiting for them.

She heard Eddie swallow hard and couldn't help but walk with an extra swing to her hips to do the dress justice. He pulled at his bow tie again.

"What you do to me, Collins," he said, resting his arm on the small of her back. She could feel the heat coming off him.

I need a few more vintage dresses like this in my collection if he appreciates it this much!

"Your highness, Ms. Collins, please follow me. I am Drew, the maître d', and I'll be your host for this evening." The man bowed.

Amanda and Eddie were so engrossed with one another's company that they hardly noticed where they were being led.

"You look so beautiful tonight, Collins," he whispered into her ear.

"Right back at you, Princey," she giggled.

The main dining room was meticulously decorated to resemble an enchanted English garden. The sight made Amanda breathless. A single table was set up in the center of the room, surrounded by plants and flowers of varying shapes and sizes, creating a delightful mix of fragrances and a burst of colors.

"This is absolutely stunning," she exclaimed as Eddie pulled out her seat. He dismissed their server, and they finally found themselves alone.

"Did you even arrange for scented candles?" Amanda asked, taking in the inviting smell of pumpkin spice and cinnamon.

"Of course. Do I leave anything half done, Collins?" Eddie replied with a smug grin, clearly pleased with her reaction. She took out her phone, captured a few photos of the room, and snapped a selfie with him.

"Eddie, you're outdone yourself. I can't believe you went to all the trouble of renting out your club," Amanda gushed, her eyes taking in every minute detail of the room.

Members-only clubs were an age-old tradition in London. It was expensive to become a member, and gaining entry into the most exclusive clubs was only possible after being introduced by an existing member.

Eddie relaxed, taking Amanda's hand in his and kissing it. "You deserve the best. If you'd allow me, I'd love to spoil you with more things, now that I know about your shopping habits."

She batted away his hand. "No, Eddie. One of the reasons I enjoy buying things is because I save up for them. I always stay within my means. Plus, I'm on a vintage kick now. You don't need to buy me anything. Actually, I'm trying to save money."

I used to shop because I liked the hard work of earning money to buy things. I mean, I wouldn't mind a piece of jewelry every once in a while, but not working has changed my outlook.

"You have no idea how incredibly attractive that makes you, Collins," Eddie said, leaning in closer.

Just as they were about to kiss, their food arrived, and the spell was broken as the scent of the oregano and basil interrupted their romantic thoughts.

"That smells absolutely divine! Do I detect spaghetti?" Amanda closed her eyes and sniffed the air.

"Yes, ma'am. Spaghetti and cloves on sundaes!" Eddie nearly jumped out of his seat in excitement.

"You remembered the Lucy reference!" Amanda said with delight.

I can't believe the level of detail he's put into tonight. First, the private club, and now, food from I Love Lucy?

In two of their favorite episodes, Lucy didn't let on that she had no idea how to speak French. When they ate out at a French restaurant one evening, Ricky and the Mertzes followed Lucy's lead by ordering at random and ended up with cloves on ice cream sundaes. The spaghetti came from an episode where Lucy had lunch at the famous Hollywood restaurant the Brown Derby.

At the Brown Derby, Lucy met the actor William Holden and was so starstruck, she stared at him as he ate. Mr. Holden then decided to return the favor and showered Lucy with the Hollywood stare. She was unable to pay attention to her food and ended up cutting her spaghetti with scissors. Lucy had the last laugh when a distracted waiter accidentally hit Bill Holden with a pie.

Amanda and Eddie tucked into their meal. She was ecstatic to discover that the cloves were actually chocolate flecks. They relished the flavors as the chocolate melted in their mouths. The food certainly exceeded her expectations.

Oh, I am never going anywhere else again. I am spoiled for life. I need the spaghetti sauce and garlic bread recipes from the chef. Talk about yummy.

Amanda took a long sip from her wineglass. "Eddie, before we go too far into dinner, I wanted to let you know that I've made a really important decision."

Eddie dabbed his mouth with a napkin. "After our disagreement the other day, I realized you were right. It's crucial that we both align our paths in life. You have my undivided attention. We can discuss anything you'd like."

Amanda toyed with the food on her plate. "It's been a long time coming, but I've decided to go back to college. I was so close to finishing the first time around. I dropped out when I had had the opportunity to become a flight attendant."

Eddie smiled at her. "That's brilliant. You have my full support. If you don't mind sharing, what were you studying at uni?"

She was curious what his reaction to her answer would be. "Math," she deadpanned.

Eddie snorted. "You are amazing, Collins. Of course you'd choose to study maths."

Amanda took a few bites of ice cream, noticing it was melting faster than she could eat it. She contemplated bringing up more about the results of her scans and the possibility of moving to London now. Eddie knew she was working for Waleeds as David's primary assistant.

However, she chose to postpone sharing any more news for now. They were nearing the end of dinner, and surgery was such a downer. She didn't want to dampen the moment.

As dinner was cleared away, Eddie stood and extended his hand, ready to lead her to the room with her next surprise.

Chapter Forty

EDDIE

Eddie's heartbeat raced, his hands growing clammy. Amanda had always been stunning, but tonight she took his breath away. He couldn't take his eyes off her the entire evening. The way her dress clung to her body, accentuating the flecks of gold in her eyes, made her seem otherworldly—like an angel.

The moment of truth was approaching. After dedicating his free time to preparing for their dance, Eddie hoped he wouldn't muck it up. The staff of Charlie's had already gone above and beyond to accommodate his last-minute requests. There were certain perks to being a royal. He knew he owed them a generous tip at the end of the evening.

I wish I had an extra day to rehearse with Clara, but here goes nothing. Amanda better not laugh at my two left feet.

Her eyes were closed. Eddie's hands trembled as he guided her toward the dance floor.

"You could have just given me a blindfold," she quipped playfully.

"No peeking!" he said, his voice wavering. He moved his hands over Amanda's eyes for an extra element of surprise.

"I'm not, I'm not," she assured as she slowly moved, with Eddie following closely behind.

He carefully guided her around any obstacles, holding his breath. "Before I remove my hands from your eyes, promise me you'll be cautious not to hurt yourself. I know you still have quite a bit of healing to do." They took a few more steps. "You can open your eyes."

"EDDIE!" Amanda squealed and jumped into his arms, and down they both went onto the floor, laughing heartily.

Ouch. Didn't expect that type of reaction. This hurts almost as much as falling off a horse. So much for her being careful.

The loud thud as they hit the wooden dance floor prompted Eddie's protection officers to rush in. "We're fine. Just a bit too much excitement. You're okay, Collins, right?"

The officers chuckled at the sight and left them alone again. Eddie made sure Amanda's delicate arm was all right before he could relax and enjoy himself. It was his first time seeing how the dancing room of Charlie's was decorated.

I don't know how they managed it, but it looks like we've walked onto a cinema set. Each room is more impressive than the last.

The room was filled with bandstands, giving the appearance that Eddie and Amanda were entering Ricky Ricardo's nightclub, the Tropicana. A few tables lay off to the side, and big band music began playing.

There wasn't a live band, but the recorded music from the club was just as good. All Amanda could do was stare and take it all in, just as he had before. Her eyes sparkled in amazement.

"A little birdy told me you've always dreamed about doing the jitterbug with King Cat Walsh. I'm not King Cat Walsh, but if you'll do me the honor of dancing with me, I intend to lead you into a swing-slash-jive." On cue, the big band music transitioned into "Stomping at the Savoy."

Amanda was speechless. A few tears escaped from her eye

and ran down her cheeks, smudging her supposedly waterproof mascara. Eddie offered his hand to her.

He felt as if an electric current ran through his body. Guiding her onto the floor, he took her waist and began leading her through the dance he had practiced only a handful of times. Her soft hands found their place around his neck.

In a trance, he gazed into her eyes and let his muscle memory take over. Time seemed to slow down. They weren't dancing at Charlie's. They were dancing at the Tropicana nightclub. He inhaled her scent, detecting notes of vanilla and orange.

Mindful of her arm, Eddie slowed his pace down and guided her through a few modified turns and steps. He savored every moment of their dance, eventually pulling her in close to his chest.

He leaned closer, his lips by her ear. In a husky voice, he softly sang a song to her. "I love Amanda, and she loves me." Amanda closed her eyes, letting the familiarity of the lyrics wash over her.

She quivered in delight in his arms. "You know, Desi wrote that song for Lucy in real life," she murmured, her voice low and quiet. "You have a beautiful singing voice, Eddie."

He leaned in closer, cupping her cheeks. "And I wrote that song for you."

He licked his lips and slowly, methodically kissed Amanda, tasting hints of chocolate on her lips. Eddie's heartbeat and breathing increased. He released her, and time resumed its normal pace. He felt the dizzying delight of what a true love's kiss must feel like. Amanda nuzzled her head into his neck as they rocked back and forth, swaying from side to side, listening to the sound of big band music from a bygone era.

Amanda placed her hand on Eddie's heart. "I can feel it through your tux. It's beating so fast."

"Now you know exactly how you make me feel."

She shivered and kissed him once more. The room seemed to grow warmer. Eddie couldn't hold himself back any longer and showed Amanda exactly what he had envisioned occurring every night in his dreams. Neither of them noticed another couple of hours slip away.

It was the early hours of the morning before they were on their way back to Kensington Palace. Instead of going directly to Clara and David's place, they decided to stop by Eddie's flat for a bit more privacy.

Wide awake after their adventurous evening and running on adrenaline, Eddie escorted Amanda there, and they made their way to the kitchen for a nightcap.

Eddie's flat had essentially been abandoned during his army tenure, yet a skeletal staff remained on-call, keeping the apartment well stocked with food and drinks in the event he stopped by.

"Eddie, this has been one of the most magical nights of my life. I want to say thank you. No man has ever done something so meaningful and considerate for me." Amanda coyly batted her lashes at him as he poured them two glasses of flavored sparkling water.

In only a few more weeks, Eddie could have the real thing. There was no way he was going to break the drinking agreement now.

"I can stay another hour before I have to be back in time for roll call," he said, raising his glass in a toast.

Amanda played with the rim of her glass, her mood shifting into hesitation.

"I wanted to let you know, I'm heading to the States for a few weeks after your graduation. I'm going to wrap everything up back home. After that, if you're okay with it, I'd like to move to London. There are some places I think I can afford in Brixton, Croydon, or out toward Balham, based on what David's paying me."

Eddie was conflicted, a whirlwind of emotions racing through his mind. "We can figure out the details of where you plan to live later. You've mentioned this to me before. You don't have to move to London. I mean, if you want to live in Seattle near your parents, we can make it work. I am forever bound to the UK, but you have a choice. Are you certain this is what you want?"

Amanda locked eyes with Eddie. "Six months ago, I would've said I can do long distance with no problems. But after the car accident, what scares me is the thought of being so far away from you. It's too long to even think about going home for a while. I'm ready to take the next step and move here to be with you. You are my world now, Eddie. Can you stand this beat-up American redhead?"

Eddie answered Amanda by carefully picking her up and spinning her around in circles as she squealed in delight. "If you can stand being around a man living in a bubble, ripe for public attack, and being an army girlfriend."

He gently placed her down, and they kissed. He caressed Amanda's cheek and pulled back, gently brushing her hair out of her face. He imprinted a mental image of her for the lonely times ahead.

Eddie moved in to cuddle her, cherishing their remaining moments together. "I may be young, but I know what I want, and Amanda Collins, I want you in my life."

He cleared his throat and began searching his pockets.

Where is it? Aha! He pulled out a small square green velvet jewelry box. *This matches her dress. Green is absolutely Amanda's color.*

It was time for the last two surprises of the evening.

"Eddie," Amanda warned. "This better not be a ring." Her mood shifted from open to guarded, and she crossed her arms.

"Come on. I'm not pulling that again." He added the word "yet" under his breath.

"Open this, and I'll explain." Eddie didn't drop down to his knees, but remained standing, carefully placing the box into her hands.

Amanda bit her lip and opened the box. Inside lay a blank silver charm in the shape of a dog bone and a red-and-blue collar with the markings of the royal family on it.

"I was hoping you might agree to becoming a furry co-parent with me. Our family dog, Franny, is about to have a litter of puppies. Should you say yes, we can make an entire list of names and spoil the puppy together."

Amanda was momentarily speechless, her eyes widening as she clapped her hands together. "Um, yes! A puppy! I haven't had a dog in years. Just another reason to move to London! What type of dog is Franny?"

Eddie's soul lit up with joy at her excitement. "Franny is an English springer spaniel. She's not a Dalmatian like your favorite Disney dogs, but she's very sweet, and once you set eyes on her, you'll never want to leave her side."

Dalmatians have to be the most hyperactive dogs out there. Should I be surprised my hyperactive girlfriend wanted a Dalmatian? Probably not.

Amanda's eyes grew watery once more. "I'm just so happy. I couldn't care less as to what breed our dog is. I want to spoil him or her rotten."

Eddie felt the corners of his eyes turning up in delight.

I've set her up. Time for the last gift.

"I have something else small for you too."

Eddie pulled out a second green velvet jewelry box. "This is your real gift from me, not our puppy's dog tag. I need to spoil both my girls."

Huh. I suppose I've declared to the universe that our puppy will be female.

Amanda opened the box, looking even more excited than before. Inside lay a small heart-shaped gold pendant on a gold chain, engraved with Eddie's signet. A dainty emerald sat in the center.

"Just a little charm so you can always have me close to you. I told you, you have my heart."

Eddie took the necklace out of the box and placed it around Amanda's neck. He lifted her hair and kissed the back of her neck, seeing goose bumps arise on her skin. She shivered in delight.

"This is too much, Eddie. I don't know if I can accept this."

"It's bespoke and made only for you. No returns or exchanges. You are stuck with it, mon ami." He laughed.

"Thank you." Amanda lifted the pendant and looked at it again in awe. "I love you, Princey. Just as you are."

"I love you too."

Eddie kissed her one last time for the evening. Their embrace was fiery and left no question in either of their minds the amount they loved one another. Eddie felt as if he could conquer the world after one of the best nights of his life.

Chapter Forty-One

EDDIE

Eddie was now in weeks fifteen and sixteen of his riding course. The previous two weeks had passed by with glacial speed. He and his group had finally been able to put everything they'd learned over the last four months together. He was eager to graduate from a recruit to a full-fledged member of the Household Cavalry Mounted Regiment, and so were the others.

But first, the troopers had one last set of tests and examinations from the cavalry's top brass. They had to demonstrate their ability to carry swords while riding and grip the four horse reins with one gauntleted hand. It was no easy feat. Their turnout was expected to be immaculate and to the highest standard yet.

Eddie could now get everything polished in just over six hours. The effort would be worth it. Polishing instilled discipline among the soldiers as they learned how to care for their horses, their uniforms, and how to keep their commanding officers happy. For a normal person, sixteen weeks would have them mastering the basics of riding a horse pretty well, but for the Army, it was considered enough time to be out on public display.

Eddie was amazed at just how far the blokes in his group had come, from putting on a saddle the incorrect way to being able to outride even him. He was proud. They were not boys anymore; they were men.

Aaron, the stocky rugby player, and once Eddie's staunchest critic, offered him a handshake on an especially late-night polishing session.

"Mate, I just wanted you to know, I don't think you're an entitled prick anymore. You're all right."

Coming from Aaron, Eddie would take his words as a compliment. "Thanks, mate."

The morning of their graduation dawned foggy and wet. It was a typical early December day in London. The recruits of Eddie's class carefully prepared their kits for the big day. Corporal Reed went through his inspection with his eagle eyes, ensuring each one of his soldiers looked smart and up to standard one last time. After this, they were on their own.

"I want each one of you boys to know how proud I am of the work you've put in. As cliché as this sounds, you have been an excellent group. Each one of you has shown tremendous grit and determination. You've been through many ups and downs and helped each other out. Continue this camaraderie. It will carry you through the darkest of times. Don't forget. Your time here in Knightsbridge will be short. You'll be able to move to field duty soon enough. Now put on a good parade for your friends and family."

The men lined up in the inner courtyard of the Knightsbridge barracks and rode out for Hyde Park on their sleek black horses. The only sounds Eddie could hear were the jingling of the horses' bridle chains, the click-clack of their hooves, and the hustle and bustle of London's traffic. This was the ultimate test.

In his full kit, Eddie sat up tall, blending seamlessly with the rest of the soldiers. Would anyone be able to pick him out of the crowd? He hoped not. The police escorts to the cavalry, the officers, and the trailing PPOs were all aware of Eddie's position. At the first sign of trouble, they would jump in. He hoped it would never come to that.

Chapter Forty-Two

AMANDA

Amanda, David, and Clara stood among the other friends and family members of the graduating recruits, lined up among the edges of one of London's most exclusive riding tracks. Members of the public peeked over the fence, capturing glimpses of the soldiers. Nothing seemed too out of the ordinary, as far as Amanda was concerned.

She couldn't take her eyes off Eddie after instantly recognizing him in the second-to-last row of the Life Guards as the class of recruits showed off their skills—walks, trots, canters, and formation changes.

Can Eddie come to me dressed like this in private? Is it sad I'm dying to try on the full uniform for myself? He said it weighs about ten pounds. It looks like a heck of a lot more.

"This brings back memories. I'm quite happy to be back here. I certainly don't miss polishing or sitting on a horse for hours on end," David said, shaking his head at the memory as they watched the parade. He looked on proudly at his cousin.

"I forget you were an army man yourself, Leeds-man. Is that why your shoes are only almost-perfectly polished? I can't even see myself in them now. What a slacker." Amanda raised her eyebrow at him.

"I'll ignore the slacker comment, as your boss," he teased back.

She laughed. "When you were in the Army, were you Blues or Reds?" she asked, filming the group to show Eddie later.

"I was in the Life Guards," David replied.

"What about Eddie's dad? He strikes me as the cavalry type." Amanda wondered if her own father would have joined the cavalry given the chance. Probably not. He was too invested in airplanes.

"Uncle Reg was a member of the Blues and Royals regiment. Eddie has actually broken with tradition. Most male members of the royal family have historically served within the Blues and Royals. Granted, Eddie had his choice of RAF, navy, marines, footguards, and King's Guard. Uncle Reg lobbied quite heavily for the cavalry. Eddie always has wanted to do things on his own terms, though."

Amanda laughed. Knowing Eddie, it didn't surprise her one bit that he had elected not to join his father's recommended regiment. She suddenly had a thought. "David, are Eddie's parents attending the parade today?"

He frowned. "Of course. They wouldn't miss Eddie's big milestone." David discreetly pointed out one of the areas of the riding track tucked a fair distance away from them and surrounded by thick foliage. "Uncle Reg and Aunt Agnus are over there. For security purposes, they wanted their attendance to be low profile. You'll be introduced to them after the ride."

Amanda's eyes widened. Knowing who Eddie's parents were and actually being introduced to them had always been two separate entities in her mind. Would they like her? Would they approve of her? Did she need to curtsy to them?

A million questions ran through her mind as the shock

slowly trickled in. Amanda forced herself to focus on watching Eddie. She would have time to panic afterward. She looked at Clara.

Her best friend's eyes were glued to the horses. "I think you're going to have to teach Amanda and me to ride, David. It looks like fun, but these horses look way too tall for me. A nice pony would do just fine."

He promised he would. Amanda had to laugh at the entire situation. If there was one person, she expected not to want anything to do with horses, it was Clara. The delicate ballerina wasn't the biggest fan of large animals.

"Collins, do you think you'll be back before New Year's Eve?" David wondered.

Amanda shrugged her left shoulder. "Depends on what the orthopedic surgeon decides. Dr. Evans is going to be looped in on the consult, and we'll go from there. I'd like to be back when Eddie's on leave." She didn't especially feel like discussing her situation on Eddie's big day.

Over the last two weeks, Amanda had pushed herself through physical therapy. The MRI scans brought in the news she was dreading—the ligament damage required surgical repair.

The surgery was already scheduled and set to take place two days from now in Los Angeles. Amanda adjusted the screen of her camera phone and made sure it stayed focused on Eddie. She bit her lip. It was one piece of news she had procrastinated telling her boyfriend.

The recruits were separating into one last formation change.

"This is the big finale," David said. They cantered past the group of onlookers in formation. The families around them let out a roar of applause at the finale. The riders didn't stop, exiting Hyde Park toward Kensington Palace.

"Eddie was bloody fantastic," Amanda cheered in a convincing British accent.

Mom has taught me well.

"Go Eddie!" Clara called out in support.

David wrapped his arms around the two ladies. "Shall we make our way over to the after-party?" Both of them eagerly agreed as Amanda clicked off her camera phone.

They were cold and ready to be nice and warm. The king had organized two big motor coaches to take all of the guests over to the palace. The Kensington Palace compound was closed to the public today for the private party.

As they boarded the bus, Amanda asked Clara, "So, um… have you been introduced to the king and queen? Any advice you can share?" They took seats near the front as David checked his email on his phone.

Clara shrugged. "The king is a lot like your dad—a military man through and through. Queen Agnus was distant. I only chatted with her for maybe two minutes. I didn't have to curtsy since it was a private meeting, or maybe because David and I had just fallen into a scummy pond." She playfully punched his shoulder.

Amanda shook her head.

"The pond…" he muttered, then cleared his throat. "Yes, well… Aunt Agnus can be a bit of an acquired taste. Once you meet her, we'll talk."

Just what were they setting her up for? Clara retold the pond story again to Amanda, who was only half-listening, her nerves getting the best of her. This was a big moment for her. How would it go?

Chapter Forty-Three

EDDIE

Eddie had done it! He was now Trooper Wales, an official full-fledged member of His Majesty's Household Cavalry Mounted Regiment!

The last few months had been grueling. At times he doubted if he could endure it until the bitter end. The friendships he had formed with Ian, Jack, Victor, and Garret were ones he hoped would last a lifetime.

"Well done, mates! We did it! We survived!" Eddie cheered as the new cavalry members stabled their horses. Out of nowhere, shot glasses and champagne appeared. "Let's have a toast and take a group photo. Who's got the longest arms for a selfie?"

Corporal Reed shook his head. "The moment the helmets come off, the recruits are transformed back into boys," he muttered. Louder, he said, "No selfies on my watch. I don't want a single excuse for trashed kits before you are presented to His Majesty. Pass me whichever mobile you want the photo on."

The group scrambled into position and took a photo.

Drinks were passed around. Everyone took their shot of champagne and followed Eddie up to the Kensington Palace presentation chambers. The king and queen awaited the arrival of their only son.

Chapter Forty-Four

AMANDA

Amanda nervously played with her hands as she followed David and Clara from the motor coach, ascending a flight of stairs to a hallway that seemed to stretch on endlessly. The lingering scent of fresh pine did little to quell her uneasy stomach, and her footsteps echoed against the black-and-white checkered marble floor.

They arrived at a pair of grand gold-gilded doors. David confidently pushed them open, revealing a small room containing a plush scarlet carpet and rich green and gold Renaissance-era tapestries. Up above, a large crystal chandelier sparkled, illuminating the windowless space.

Amanda gulped. On the far side of the room, positioned next to two red antique-looking thrones, stood Eddie's parents —the king and queen. Their quiet conversation abruptly stopped as they noticed David, Amanda, and Clara enter the room.

Approaching the monarchs, Amanda observed the king, dressed in a navy-blue military dress uniform, standing just slightly shorter than David. His balding sandy hair and blue eyes led her to wonder if this was a glimpse of what Eddie might look like as he aged. He had a stockier build than his son.

Her gaze shifted to the queen. Her light brown hair was pulled back into a severe updo, and her posture was rigid. It was evident she did not approve of either American. The queen's eyes bore into Amanda, studying her like a lion studying its prey. Her stomach muscles tightened, but she resisted the urge to flinch and maintained her gaze, even as others in the room seemed to pay them no attention.

David greeted his aunt and uncle with a warm smile. "Uncle Reg, Aunt Agnus, as always, it's good see you." King Reginald beamed, in contrast to the queen, who offered a subdued half smile.

"David, an excellent ceremony, wasn't it? Edmund was in fine form," the king said animatedly. "Ah, Miss Little, how wonderful to see you."

Clara stepped forward, exchanging handshakes with the king. "Likewise, Your Highness."

The queen adhered to formal protocol and inclined her head. "Miss Little." Clara appeared unaffected by the reception as she stepped back and returned to David's side.

The king's attention shifted to Amanda, and David proceeded with the introductions. "Uncle, Aunt, I'm pleased to be the one to formally introduce you to Miss Amanda Collins."

"Well, Miss Collins. I daresay it is about time we make your acquaintance." Amanda began to curtsy, but the king intervened, insisting, "None of that, my dear. We aren't so formal in private," as he shook hands firmly with her.

As with Clara, the queen nodded to Amanda in acknowledgment. "Miss Collins."

Regardless of the reception, Amanda found herself at a loss for words. She stared wide-eyed at the couple. It took a few moments for the shock to subside. Meanwhile, Clara,

David, and the king kept the conversation flowing, and she observed quietly.

It's the king and queen. I knew this was coming, but wow. Adrenaline flooded Amanda's body. Slowly, some of the nervous tension abated. *It's just Eddie's parents. They're just like my mom and dad. Kind of. Not really.*

The queen interrupted Amanda's thoughts, asking, "Miss Collins, would you mind indulging me in a private word?" She didn't wait for Amanda's response and stepped away from the earshot of David, Clara, and the king.

Amanda took a deep breath and followed. The queen began. "Miss Collins, I see you are the latest woman to capture my son's romantic interest. Edmund has always had a certain rebellious nature about him."

How should she respond to that? The queen was bordering on rude. Perhaps she was testing her, echoing what David had hinted at earlier.

Despite her shaking hands, Amanda kept her tone cool and voiced her response as calmly as she could. "Yes, I am the woman Eddie is dating. I consider myself incredibly fortunate to have him in my life."

The queen considered her answer. "As this is the very beginning of our acquaintance, let me be quite clear with you. I don't approve of you dating my son. Americans have no place in the British monarchy. Edmund will have many responsibilities in the years to come. In this family, duty is put above our personal lives. We devote ourselves to the service of the country."

Amanda was surprised to find herself appreciating the directness of the queen, but a slow anger simmered to the surface. Keeping her tone respectful, she said, "I understand, Your Majesty. Growing up in a military family, I was taught from an early age exactly what duty and honor mean."

She paused and took a breath. "You may not approve of

me, but know this: I love your son. Regardless of where our relationship takes us, I will always support Eddie and whatever path he needs to follow. Also, just so you are aware, my mother is English. Not that it should matter, but I'm not just an American citizen, I'm also a British subject."

Amanda held a steady gaze on her. Then the queen slowly blinked and offered her a genuine smile.

"I'm happy we understand one another. My son and daughter mean everything. Their happiness is of the utmost importance to Reginald and me. Despite my reservations, I would be a fool to stand in Edmund's way. I may not approve of you, but that doesn't mean you won't change my mind in the future. Now it's high time we celebrated Edmund's graduation."

They rejoined the group. Clara shot Amanda a questioning glance, but Amanda shook her head. She could fill in her best friend later. Standing before the queen, she had summoned enough strength and confidence to surprise even herself. The moment had passed, leaving her feeling drained of energy. However, this was Eddie's day, and she was here to celebrate it.

The door to the presentation chamber swung open once more as Eddie made his entrance, adorned in a complete ceremonial cavalry uniform.

Chapter Forty-Five

EDDIE

Eddie grinned from ear to ear. His large boots created a thud as he walked across the room. He exchanged warm greetings, kissing his mother and hugging his father, David, Clara, and Amanda. Discreetly, the trio stepped aside, allowing him a few moments of precious privacy with his parents. They knew they only had a brief interval before they would need to rejoin the rest of the graduates and their families.

Eddie's father exuded excitement, his eyes bright with pride as he looked on at his son. "Edmund! A remarkable display of horsemanship. I'm so very proud of you, son. You looked like a seasoned soldier. How long have you been on that particular mount?"

Eddie removed his helmet and scratched his head. "Thank you, Father. I've been riding Acton for about five days now. I'm hoping my favorite mount, Freddy, becomes available for me to ride again soon. We got on well."

The king absorbed the information. "I've heard you were named the top recruit in the Ride. Congratulations are in order. Clearly, you've inherited your skills from my side of the family," he added.

The queen chose to overlook her husband's remark. "Regardless of who you received your riding skills from, we are extremely pleased with how far you've come. I promised myself I wouldn't cry, but you really have blossomed into a wonderful young man."

His mother hid a few tears. Eddie's own eyes grew watery. He hugged her close. "Thanks, Mum."

Next he pulled Amanda aside for a private greeting, hugging her tightly and giving her a kiss. She pulled back, admiring his uniform, "I am soooooooo prooooooud of you," she purred, her eyes sparkling as she looked at him. Eddie felt a surge of pride, standing a little taller under her appreciative gaze.

The king cleared his throat, and Eddie and Amanda jumped apart. "Miss Collins, I forgot to mention it earlier, but please convey to your family that the invitation for all of you to join us up in Sandringham for Christmas still stands if you change your plans. The queen and I understand you may need some time to recover after your procedure. My best wishes, and do keep my staff informed if there's anything we can do to assist you." Amanda's eyes widened at the offer.

Eddie frowned, puzzled. What procedure? As far as he knew, Amanda's trip home was planned to see her parents for Christmas. He studied her, trying to discern if anything had changed since their date two weeks prior.

"What am I missing?" he asked, louder than intended.

She shot him a look that said they'd talk about it later.

"Edmund, did you have a question? Speak up," his father prompted.

Eddie winced. His father didn't take to having one-off, private conversations like his mother.

"Nothing, Father. I just need to speak with Amanda privately," he responded.

The king nodded, accepting his answer. "Well then, I'll leave you two alone. I'll expect you in the reception area in two minutes. We're long overdue."

Eddie took Amanda by the hand and guided her to the side of the thrones.

"You're having surgery?"

She nodded. "I thought it wouldn't be until after Christmas, but the specialist in Seattle had a cancellation come up, so I decided to take it," she said sheepishly, looking at him. "I can explain."

Eddie couldn't divert his gaze from her.

So this is what she's been hiding.

"I knew it was a possibility, but why didn't you tell me?" His voice wavered, revealing his hurt feelings.

"I didn't mean for you to find out this way. I didn't want to take away from your big day. Today is about celebrating all your hard work. Don't worry about me," Amanda said, her voice trembling. The fear and moisture in her eyes hit Eddie like a punch to the gut.

His anger and disappointment surged in his chest. "But I do worry about you. This is a big deal. There should be no secrets between us! Are there other things you're keeping from me?" Eddie shook his head. He couldn't do this now. "No, don't answer that. I have to go."

I need to focus my energy on introducing the blokes to my dad.

Amanda's shoulders hunched, and her voice carried an air of weariness. "Why not just discuss this now? It's surgery at home. That's all, I swear."

Eddie let out a frustrated huff. He was trying to give her the attention she deserved, not simply dismiss her. Besides, he didn't trust himself not to say something he'd regret.

"Edmund!" his father bellowed.

"I have to go." Eddie hurriedly rushed over to the waiting king and queen, unable to meet her eyes.

Chapter Forty-Six

AMANDA

"I can see I was wrong. I was going to tell you later today. Don't put this all on me, Edmund," Amanda whispered to the empty thrones.

I'm the one who should be worrying. Can't there be one moment for you to celebrate your hard work? I don't want to be the Debbie Downer. For once, I'm trying to protect you instead of the other way around.

Amanda needed space. She couldn't bear to be near the joyful presence of David and Clara. The painful expression of hurt on Eddie's face crushed her. She fled the empty presentation room, her footsteps echoing loudly. Her pulse quickened.

Reaching the reception area, she could hear the clinking of glasses, laughter, and light banter from within, amplifying her darkened state of mind. After three months of so many ups and downs on her emotional roller coaster, Amanda had finally reached her limit. She felt shattered. Tightness gripped her chest, and she began to struggle for breath.

I... am... having... an... anxiety... attack... need... air... need... to... be... outside.

Amanda sprinted outside as fast as she could, leaving

everything behind. She released her frustrations through tears, letting them flow freely into the wind as her hair came tumbling down. Along the way, she lost her shoes.

Running was her solace. The cold wind whipped past her, and the world blurred into a hazy rush. All that existed were the elements of nature, the rushing air, and her own heavy breathing. She didn't stop until she couldn't push herself any farther. She dropped to her hands and knees, startling a few ducks on an empty grassy knoll across from a pond.

It was tranquil and misty. The only sounds around her were the flapping of wings, soothing flowing water, and distant children's laughter. A thin blanket of fog enshrouded her. The cold, solid ground provided a welcome relief to her overly warm body. The fragrance of flowers lingered in the air. Amanda closed her eyes and attempted to take several deep breaths. She wept until there were no more tears left to shed.

Goose bumps formed on her skin. Her arm ached, her feet ached, everything ached. She stared out into the mist and curled up into a ball. She scolded herself for impulsively flee-ing. In the depths of her mind, Amanda acknowledged that she'd acted childishly and recklessly by running away and wallowing in self-pity.

Why had she decided to lie on the ground? Her shoulder was still extremely tender. Slowly, she sat up, pulled her knees to her chest, and rested her head on them. She had no idea how long she sat in the grass as she sniffled.

Heavy hoof beats and the sound of a panting horse drew nearer and nearer. She looked up.

"Amanda?" Eddie's voice echoed. "Amanda, where are you?" His tone bordered on hysterical as the galloping approached.

"I'm here," she called out into the mist. Ten feet away, she made out Eddie's figure clad in his cavalry tunic and boots, riding a broad brown thoroughbred. Spotting her, he urged his mount over. As the horse approached, Eddie leaped off and sprinted to her. He dropped down onto his knees, and Amanda felt his hot breath as he frantically stripped out of his tunic and wrapped it around her shoulders.

"You are freezing. What were you thinking?" He rubbed her limbs, attempting to warm her.

"I'm sorry," was all she managed to say, shivering. Eddie pulled her closer to his body as they both sat on the ground. Amanda closed her eyes and soaked in the warmth from his hard ride.

"I'm sorry too. I overreacted when you mentioned the surgery. The moment you ran out, I realized we should've spoken about it straightaway. I would have been here sooner, but I needed a horse to keep up with you. I can't move fast enough in these jackboots. You're quite the runner." Eddie continued to rub Amanda's arms and back.

"We were both dumb. I was procrastinating. Every time I was going to tell you, I found an excuse. Today, the way you looked at me broke me. I couldn't handle the hurt, so I ran." Amanda repositioned the tunic over her cold body.

Eddie broke apart from her and helped her up into a kneeling position. "I was trying to shield you from my anger. I've worked hard learning to control my emotions. When I felt it welling up, I didn't want to take it out on you. I tried to distance myself until I had calmed down."

Amanda hugged him tightly and tenderly. "In hindsight, that would have been a better way to handle this. I bottled up all my emotions for months, and the dam finally burst. I need to learn from you, Princey."

Both Amanda and Eddie stood. Not wanting to waste a single moment, they kissed with an urgent need to ensure they were both all right. Amanda felt Eddie's stubble brush over her face. She leaned into him, feeling safe and protected. Loved.

My prince.

Several jabs of pain in her shoulder signaled to both of them it was time to return to the palace.

"But before we go any further, we need to get you inside and warmed up. What happened to your shoes? You know what, don't even answer that. I don't need to know."

Eddie scooped Amanda up in his arms and carried her over to his horse. Gently positioning her onto his mount, he slid onto the saddle behind her and rode them over the threshold back toward Kensington Palace.

Chapter Forty-Seven

AMANDA

It was another bright, sunny day in Southern California as Amanda entered the guest room closet of her apartment one last time and directed Eddie to retrieve the remaining box from the top shelf.

She felt a sense of accomplishment for overseeing the packing of her place during the three weeks she'd been back to the States. She had to admit, Eddie's security team had done an excellent job vacuuming, painting, and cleaning. Even the kitchen appliances were gleaming!

She was returning her apartment in much better shape than she had received it, and she was sure to get her security deposit back without any issues.

After calling Southern California her home for a few years, Amanda was still coming to terms with moving to London. Many of the boxes she'd packed would be heading straight to Eddie's Kensington Palace flat. Larger items would be sent to Seattle.

"That's the last of it. Is this one a keeper too?" Eddie asked.

Amanda glanced at her pile of boxes for recycling.

I can't believe how many boxes and shopping bags I've kept for the packaging. There has to be close to fifty if you add in all of the cosmetic ones. Even after selling a good amount of my clothes and accessories, it's amazing what I have amassed over the years. Maybe I need to consider the minimalist route.

"You can recycle the Coach box. There isn't really anything too special about it other

than I liked the size," Amanda said with a smile as she looked on.

Her apartment held so many memories—good, bad, and ugly. This was the first place she had lived on her own and learned the ropes of adulting. She never did get her porch swing, but Eddie had promised to have one installed before she arrived home in London.

"Is there a reason my name is written on this box?" Eddie, about to put the box into the recycle pile, started to pry the lid off.

Amanda squinted. Which box did he have?

She inhaled sharply. *Oh no… my scrapbook! If Eddie finds out what's in there, I'll never hear the end of it. Knowing about it is one thing; actually seeing it is another.*

"Oh, that box doesn't have anything in it." Amanda casually moved closer to him, attempting to reach it. "But on second thought, I better look through it just in case."

"No way. There's something important in here, isn't there?" Eddie gleefully held it high out of Amanda's reach and ran around the room as she chased him.

"No, that's not fair. You're like two feet taller than me. Give it here." Amanda huffed and jumped, reaching for it with her good arm.

Three weeks after rotator cuff surgery, she was eager to return to normal. She hoped that by the four-week mark, she'd be able to lose the sling. The procedure had gone well, and she was already ahead of schedule, as confirmed by her surgeon.

"No such thing. Finders keepers," Eddie teased, darting behind his human shield, Jonathan.

Amanda appealed to the head PPO. "Wanna help a girl out here?" She sent a glare to Eddie.

"I'm sorry, Ms. Collins. I'm staying out of this one." Jonathan stepped out of the way and she decided getting the box wasn't worth the effort.

"Fine. Keep the dumb box." She stuck her tongue out at Eddie, who laughed her off.

He moved closer to her. "Time to see what treasure awaits me." Eddie carefully pulled the box open. Amanda braced herself for the coming banter.

"This is the famous Prince of Wales scrapbook!" he exclaimed, picking up the well-worn lacy photo album with his family crest on the front. He opened it and flipped through a couple of pages. His cheeks turned rosy pink as he quickly shut it. "On second thought, I have no desire to relive my teenage years and awkward body-slash-partying ways in photos again. Once was enough."

Amanda crossed her arms. "Serves you right." She retrieved the album and tucked it under her arm for safe-keeping.

Eddie looks so adorable when he's embarrassed. These twin patches of pink make him look just like the doll I have. I hope he never discovers that!

"Don't be too embarrassed. It's even more satisfying to know you've had your eye on me for a long time." He moved to stand next to her and pecked her cheek.

She cleared her throat, not eager to elaborate. "If you wouldn't mind, can you please put this in my backpack? I'll find a new spot for it later near my Prince Edmund calendar."

Eddie thankfully changed the subject. "Southern California is the perfect place to visit, but I'm more than happy to return to the UK. I'll never be able to understand how to tolerate the traffic. It's a living nightmare."

He picked up the forgotten Coach box and passed it off to Jonathan, making sure it was indeed going to be recycled. "I think that about does it, Collins. Are you ready to take another round of meds?" He glanced at his watch, his tone becoming more serious.

Amanda took stock of how she was feeling. "I think I'm gonna skip it today, Princey. I feel pretty good. It's the first time in about a week that my pain is down to a dull throb."

"Are you positive? No whining if you change your mind." Eddie crossed his arms, meaning business.

"Yup. Definitely able to skip it. Let's celebrate. I think everybody is ready for some BBQ Shack. The moving van is due at about one this afternoon. After that, we can head to the hotel." Amanda's mention of the BBQ Shack grabbed the attention of all the men in her apartment, causing them to pause momentarily and stop what they were doing, then hustle at a quicker pace.

Eddie may employ these guys, but I still hold power with the magic words. Hehe. Feels good to be in charge.

"BBQ Shack! I'm getting an extra-large order of chips," Eddie boasted.

Chapter Forty-Eight

EDDIE

"I never got a chance to thank you for giving up your hard-earned leave to come and help me move, Eddie," Amanda said from the back seat of his rented car as they enjoyed their lunch. Her VW had already been sent to Seattle.

He reached over to steal the remnants of her shake. "I don't mind escaping the cold of London at all. It's quite nice to be in America. How did you manage to convince your parents to spend the holidays at Sandringham with us?"

"Oh. That was easy. I told them I was still considering between finishing my undergrad degree at Christ Church College in Oxford or University College in London. I said I needed to see both campuses and meet with the staff. David sweetened the deal by mentioning Waleeds is going to offer me a scholarship. Dad stopped trying to talk me into the University of Washington after that." Amanda snatched the shake back from Eddie's hands.

"I know your mum was pushing Oxford. Would it help if I told you I favor UCL?" Eddie chuckled.

Amanda reached over and this time stole his discarded army jacket. "Not at all. I'm making my own well-informed decisions. I've been emailing some of the prospective professors I might be working with. Both schools have great reputations, but UCL holds a slight lead over Oxford for logistical purposes. If I'm going to be living at your place, it's a lot easier for me to reach the UCL campus."

"So you've finally decided to move in with me after all the pleading and begging I had to do? It's nice to know my efforts paid off," Eddie teased.

She punched him lightly in the arm. "Don't get too big-headed. London is expensive and I'd like to put away some of what I earn each month. Daddy and your father have made it clear they want a secure location for me. We've been looking into flats around London, but the press has been on to us. I don't feel right having to subject the neighborhood to their craziness."

Eddie didn't care. Amanda was coming to London, and she was going to be moving in with him!

The press. I'll never be rid of them. He sighed. *I guess it helps that I spend the majority of my time at the Knightsbridge Barracks. Amanda is essentially house-sitting for me.*

Eddie's mind turned to their new role as furry parents. Their new puppy wasn't going to take long to settle in. He hoped David and Clara were prepared to assist.

It's going to be challenging to housebreak a puppy. His eyes wandered to Amanda's relaxed form. *She looks so cozy in my jacket.*

"Have I ever told you how proud of you I am and how much I love you?" he asked her playfully.

"Maybe once or twice, but you had better refresh my memory about how amazing of a kisser you are."

Amanda's lips crashed into Eddie's before he was ready,

leaving him breathless and eager for more. She slid into his lap as he carefully wrapped his arms around her.

"Much better." Amanda rested on her human pillow as they waited for the security team to finish eating their own meals. Life as boyfriend and girlfriend couldn't get much better than this.

Epilogue

AMANDA

Amanda stepped out into the sunshine from the Westminster Underground station, relishing the warmth of the early afternoon sun. Not far behind her, three burly security men discreetly dressed as tourists followed.

She had to give herself credit—with the brown pixie haircut wig and sunglasses, she really didn't resemble herself. It had thrown off any nosy reporters. With her headphones in, Amanda enjoyed the music of the Beatles as she walked toward Horse Guards Parade.

The bell of Big Ben went off twelve times, signaling the noon hour. Most Londoners, as she had come to find out, set their watches to the famous clock. It was a marvelous sound to hear it ring out. In the Whitehall area of London, tourists seemed to be everywhere.

Amanda soaked in the sight of them lining up near her intended destination. Slightly lowering her shades, she looked to see two British Cavalry members on black horses in the sentry box, on duty.

A line of people eagerly waited to have the opportunity to

get their photos taken next to the horses, even with the sign "Horses May Kick or Bite" on the box's wall next to them. With the white plumed helmet and red tunic, Eddie blended in with the other members of his regiment.

Funny, there are more police than usual out and about and not a single person seems to notice the extra security around.

She waited for the signal to turn from red to green, then crossed to join the line of tourists.

In what had become a daily ritual, a disguised Amanda stopped by Horse Guards Parade anytime Eddie was on sentry duty to see if she could fool him. So far, she was ten for twenty.

She grinned when it was her turn to be next to him. Her heart skipped a few beats. She felt a magnetic pull toward him. His horse, Freddy, knew her well and nuzzled her on the shoulder.

Amanda gently ran her hand over the horse's muzzle. "Way to give it away today."

Her wig slipped as she attempted to take a selfie. She repositioned it. Her previously injured arm was finally free of its sling. How wonderful it felt to be able to use it again almost normally.

"Would you like me to take your photo, ma'am?" one of her security team members inquired. Amanda schooled her face into one of surprise.

"Yes, please. If you wouldn't mind." She moved in as close as she dared to Eddie and Freddy and posed for the camera.

"Thank you, soldier." She saluted and moved out of the queue. Amanda was well aware Eddie wouldn't be able to move from his place or greet her, but the minute upturn of his eyes gave her the only message she needed.

Turning on her heel, she marched in the opposite direction from where she had come from, heading toward Buckingham Palace. Eddie would win today's round. She always looked forward to their text messages between his stints of guard duty in the sentry box.

With the royal wedding rapidly approaching and her never-ending load of advanced calculus, this was the only time Amanda seemed to have to herself anymore. She wouldn't trade it for the world.

She whistled a tune that sounded something like "I Want to Hold Your Hand" from the Beatles as she greeted the guard and went through the private entrance of the palace. After dating Eddie for a few months the palace guards could distinguish Amanda and her security detail on sight. She slipped inside and took the familiar route to see Francine and her litter of six exceedingly hyper English springer spaniels.

"How's our girl doing today?" Amanda gushed, finding the smallest puppy of the litter and picking her up. The puppy, who had yet to be named, happily sniffed her and began licking her face. She laughed in delight.

"Well, it's good to see you too. Eddie can't make it, but that doesn't stop me from spoiling you. Who's the little princess? You are!"

Placing the puppy down to join its siblings, Amanda couldn't help herself and ensured all the puppies received equal attention.

"I see you've stopped in to spoil the lot yet again, Ms. Collins." King Reginald entered his study dressed for riding, smiling at the sight before him.

"Your Highness! I didn't think you were in today. I'm so sorry for interrupting. I was just heading down to the kitchens to make a late lunch for my team." Amanda stood, brushing her jeans off and turning her attention from the puppies to the king.

"We've discussed this before," he said, giving her a knowing look.

She hesitated. "I'm sorry, Reggie. It still doesn't seem right to call you by your first name. At least do the same for me, please."

"Forgive me, Amanda. To answer your earlier question, you weren't interrupting me at all. Although my staff is not as popular as you these days, why not let them handle lunch? I'm sure your team will be in capable hands. Why not join me for a ride, and we can discuss proper names for the young pups." The king's suggestion didn't really leave any room to maneuver.

Amanda bit her lip. *I'm really not dressed for riding, and I'm not confident on horses.*

"Reggie, I'm still new to riding. I'm not sure I'm ready to upgrade from my pony yet."

The king's eyes sparkled. "I don't expect you to be an expert rider, but indulge an old man. I promise I won't let anything happen to you. I know a thing or two about riding." He winked playfully. "Did I mention that Alice is here? She's quite excited to see you."

Princess Alice, Eddie's sister, was one of the sweetest and shyest people Amanda had ever encountered. Appearance-wise, she was the female version of Eddie.

At fifteen, Alice had shoulder-length blonde hair, blue eyes, and was about five foot four. She was an excellent horse-woman and tennis player. Amanda had only begun to help her open up. Having a mutual love for outdoor activities helped. They were quickly becoming friends.

She relented. "All right, but only if you promise we can go really slow."

The king nodded in confirmation. "Excellent, you ring your team, and I'll call down to the stables." He lowered his voice. "It's the last place Lottie will find us."

Just as they were about to step out of the king's study, Princess Charlotte, David's mother, entered the room.

"There you two are. Perfect timing. I have a few things I wanted to run by you. Can you look at this seating chart?" Amanda and the king exchanged looks.

Neither one wanted to upset the Princess Royal. With the wedding so close, she was even worse than ever at confirming the minutest of details.

I took care of her last time.

Inspiration struck her. "Charlotte, great timing. Reggie and I have Francine and her puppies gathered. I think it's the perfect moment to fit them for those adorable little bow ties you mentioned."

Amanda subtly edged toward the door. *Take the bait. Sorry, Franny.* The royal family's dog looked up and gave her sad eyes.

David's mother nodded. "I'd completely forgotten. Excellent catch, Amanda."

"Right then, Lottie, I have an important meeting requiring Ms. Collins and then a meeting with Lord Renbrook. Please excuse us." The king and Amanda slowly left the room, each quickening their pace away from the Princess Royal.

"Good save. Let's ride out as far as we possibly can before she finds us again," Amanda called out.

~

Six Months Later

Eddie and Amanda had a rare weekend together. It was late afternoon. Amanda drew back the sheer white curtains of room 2403, the Sleeping Beauty Suite. Eddie had surprised her with her first trip to Disneyland Paris and, naturally, had booked the largest suite in the hotel.

Situated on a private floor, it offered a stunning view of Main Street, USA, leading up to the iconic pink and blue castle. Each time they stepped into the room, Amanda had to pinch herself in disbelief.

She opened the double glass doors to the private balcony, removing the mouse-shaped ears from her head and resting her elbows against the railing. The scent of fresh cinnamon churros wafted up to them.

I could've used one of those ten minutes ago.

They had just finished their afternoon tea, having already explored Disney Village and seen most of the Hollywood Studios Park. Eddie and the team had all agreed on a break and some refreshments before conquering Disneyland Park.

Eddie settled at the suite's piano and began playing "When You Wish Upon a Star." Amanda sang the words softly to herself, relishing in the mellow music.

Eddie is really gifted. I wish he would showcase his musical talents more.

Stepping back inside, she stood next to the grand piano. He moved into the next song, "A Whole New World" from Aladdin. She began singing the lyrics, encouraging him to join her.

Eyes closed, he played and sang from memory. It was a favorite Disney movie of theirs. When he hit the last chord, he looked up from the piano bench at Amanda.

Then Eddie got down on one knee. She gasped, her hands flying to her mouth, heart pounding in her ears. "YES!" she screamed.

He shook his head. "I haven't even asked you yet, A. Let me do this the right way."

Amanda bit her lip, struggling to contain her laughter and maintain her composure.

Remaining on one knee, Eddie retrieved a black ring box from his jeans pocket and opened it. He took a deep breath, his expression serious. "Amanda, a year and a half ago, you walked into my life. You're unlike any woman I've ever met. Your personality is vibrant, and you possess kindness, compassion, and care like no one else. I love you beyond measure, to the ends of the earth and back. Will you honor me by becoming my princess?"

Amanda was giddy. She bounced up and down, barely able to contain her excitement. "YES!" she shouted again.

Eddie rose, slid the emerald and diamond ring onto her finger, then swept her off her feet, gently dipping her. They shared a passionate kiss. Amanda was breathless, feeling his warm breath against her cheek.

The door to the suite swung open as Jonathan peeked inside. They pulled away from each other and she giggled. "I take it your mission was a success, sir?"

"Absolutely! Amanda said yes." Eddie beamed, showing him the ring.

Jonathan produced two champagne flutes and a chilled bottle from behind his back. "Time to celebrate!"

Eddie and Amanda kissed again.

Dreams do come true.

Dear Reader

Thank you for taking the time to read "Jiving With a Royal."

If you enjoyed this book, please take a moment to leave a review on Amazon, Goodreads, Bookbub, or whatever platform you may have discovered this book on. It helps Tomi connect with readers like you!

Love her books? Become a part of her treasured community here.

Stay connected with Tomi by scanning QR code, or by visiting her official website.

Https://TomiTabb.com

Acknowledgments

There have been so many people who have helped make these books possible.

I'd like to first acknowledge my editing and design team—Kaylee Baldwin, Ranee Clark, and Joanne Lui. Thank you ladies, without you, literally none of these characters would be here today. From the bottom of my heart, thank you so very much for everything.

To my beta readers and proofreaders, especially Erin and Charity, thank you for the countless hours you've been looking over and reviewing my work.

To my rainy day partner-in-crime, fellow author Brooke Gilbert thank you for all of your constant support and lending me your time and input. The new covers you have designed for my royals books are beyond stunning!

To my readers, thank you for continuing to support my writing journey. With each story I tell, I feel as if I become a stronger writer.

To my family, thank you so much for your constant love and support. I know how difficult it can be to work around my schedule. Please know how much I appreciate your flexibility!

About the Author

Tomi Tabb writes closed-door romantic comedies filled with heart, hope, and happily-ever-afters. From royalty and bodyguards to engineers, athletes, and performers, her stories celebrate kindness, found family, and the joy of falling in love. Inspired by *Pride and Prejudice*, Tomi writes the character-driven romances she loves to read—equal parts swoony, hopeful, and satisfying.

A California native, Tomi holds an MA in History and is putting the finishing touches on her doctorate in History, blending her love of research with her passion for storytelling. She lives with her family, one very spoiled cat, and an energetic toddler who keeps life wonderfully unpredictable.

When she isn't writing, you'll likely find her figure skating, watching tennis, or hunting down the newest pumpkin-flavored treat—one of the many reasons fall will always be her favorite season.

Website: TomiTabb.com